GUNNING FOR TROUBLE

Two relentless forces were at work in the Principe range, and Wade Forrest was caught between them. Wade's gun made too much trouble for Deac Shanter, ramrod of the T Anchor, and he was ordered to drift by sundown.

But along the trail, Arne Bassett had posted his gunhawks to see that Forrest never made it out of the country alive with secrets that would ruin the rancher.

No matter how he turned, his number was up—and, in the time it takes to load a .44, Wade had to decide which man should have first crack at killing him!

L(eonard) L(ondon) Foreman was born in London, England in 1901. He served in the British army during the Great War, prior to his emigration to the United States. He became an itinerant, holding a series of odd jobs in the western States as he traveled. He began his writing career by introducing his most widely known and best-loved character, Preacher Devlin, in "Noose Fodder" in *Western Aces* (12/34), a pulp magazine. Throughout the mid thirties, this character, a combination gunfighter, gambler, and philosopher, appeared regularly in *Western Aces*. Near the end of the decade, Foreman's Western stories began appearing in Street & Smith's *Western Story Magazine*, where the pay was better. Foreman's first Western novels began appearing in the 1940s, largely historical Westerns such as *Don Desperado* (1941) and *The Renegade* (1942). The *New York Herald Tribune* reviewer commented on *Don Desperado* that "admirers of the late beloved Dane Coolidge better take a look at this. It has that same all-wool-and-a-yard-wide quality." Foreman continued to write prolifically for the magazine market as long as it lasted, before specializing exclusively for the book trade with one of his finest novels, *Arrow in the Dust* (1954) which was filmed under this title the same year. Two years earlier *The Renegade* was filmed as *The Savage* (Paramount, 1952), the two are among several films based on his work. Foreman's last years were spent living in the state of Oregon. Perhaps his most popular character after Preacher Devlin was Rogue Bishop, appearing in a series of novels published by Doubleday in the 1960s. George Walsh, writing in *Twentieth Century Western Writers*, said of Foreman: "His novels have a sense of authority because he does not deal in simple characters or simple answers." In fact, most of his fiction is not centered on a confrontation between good and evil, but rather on his characters and the changes they undergo. His female characters, above all, are memorably drawn and central to his stories.

GUNNING FOR TROUBLE

L. L. Foreman

GUNSMOKE

This hardback edition 2008
by BBC Audiobooks Ltd
by arrangement with
Golden West Literary Agency

ISBN 978 1 405 68212 1

British Library Cataloguing in Publication Data available.

Printed and bound in Great Britain by
CPI Antony Rowe, Chippenham, Wiltshire

CHAPTER 1

THE NOON stage jingled into Maya dead on time after running the long loops down through the North Principe, and drew in at Toland's Hotel on the east side of the wide street. Booting the brake, the driver swung his head toward the Saturday crowd on the hotel gallery. His heavily meaningful look signaled, "This is him!"

So it was known here, as it had been at Arco and all the stops farther north for a hundred miles or more. Wade Forrest reached for his warbag and stepped down onto the boardwalk. He caught the driver's mute message and observed with a stale irritation the curiosity of the gallery shaders. All the way down from Arco, sharing the driver's seat, he had walled off conversation leading to himself. But it was plain that the driver already knew. Like most of his kind he soaked up news like a blotter and passed it on at the first chance. It was expected of him.

Glancing down after his fare, the driver kicked off the brake and whistled to his horses. The stage half-circled across the street to Wright's Livery for fresh teams before making the long run straight on down the South Principe and through Black Walls, to make connection with the Ute City stage line.

Wade Forrest gave his bag to the hotel clerk at the door and followed him in. "Number nine," the clerk said. "Back room, all we got left. Always full, Sa'days."

"All right." He signed, but didn't go up to the room.

Low-toned voices broke off as he emerged from the cool gloom of the lobby. He guessed the loungers had been discussing him and would inspect his name on the register for corroboration of the stage driver's wink. The tired irritation returned. He raked a deliberate glance over each man on the gallery, but could discover nothing

5

of promise. Their faces assumed solemn vacancy. No stare of threat met him. He turned from them, his tension loosening, to examine the wide street. Soon locating what he sought, he left the hotel gallery and crossed the street at an angle to the west side, patiently avoiding the traffic of rigs and horsemen.

The Sheriff's office stood at the corner of West Block and West Street. Wade entered the open door under the faded sign and nodded to the man he found inside.

"My name's Forrest."

"I'm Stuart."

"I know."

Sheriff Stuart resembled an elderly bartender off duty. He wore a baggily respectable black suit, a low-crowned hat on the back of his bald head, a huge silver watch chain and a faded pink necktie. He was short, pudgy. His thick mustache stayed untidy despite his constantly stroking thumb. He smoked cigars in an imitation amber holder, the gold-dipped band of which had long ago turned to brass.

But Stuart's eyes had depth and his reputation ran far afield of Maya and Principe Valley. This man had rammed the law into the toughest places of the Southwest, with a nickel-plated pistol carried loosely in his coat pocket and a way of ambling up to a lawbreaker and requesting him to come along. As Sheriff in an average cowtown he called himself retired.

"Don't get up," Wade said. "I'll sit."

Stuart smiled faintly, waiting for him to drag up the only other chair and get seated. He stretched a lazy hand over the battered desk. Wade shook it briefly, sensing the cold friendlessness of the grip, liking the man for not sugaring it. He dipped into his shirt pocket and pulled out a small black gutta-percha case. He pressed the catch and opened it, exposing a fold of paper and a miniature picture, an ambrotype. He slid the case onto the desk before the Sheriff.

"Ever seen her?"

Stuart examined the picture thoroughly. He touched a stubby finger to the paper and raised an inquiring glance.

"Description," Wade said.

Stuart unfolded the paper. He read aloud, "Height,

about five-two. Weight, hunnerd-an'-five. Dark hair.
Dark blue eyes. Skin, fair. Age, nineteen. Pretty. H'm
. . . no name here."

"Name doesn't matter," Wade said.

"No, guess not." Stuart folded the paper back carefully
in its creases. He looked again at the picture of the girl.
"Pretty little thing." Pushing the case back over the desk,
he stated definitely, "She ain't here. Sorry."

His aging eyes contained nothing of the secret mirth
that most males felt for a man whose girl had skipped.
Passion and malice were ironed out of him and he knew
that what was hurtful was never funny.

"I've narrowed it down to here," Wade murmured.
He stared musingly at the gutta-percha case, his head
bowed slightly, a stubbornly insistent man.

Stuart shook his bald head slowly. "Look, Forrest. We
all know about this. Everybody. It's the talk of every
gabby stage driver, your stopping off every place, asking
about her, showing her picture. You think she could be
here and not get spotted? 'Small, dark, and pretty.' Man,
it's already a kind of saying, a joke. We've been hearing
about you nearly a month now." Then, his eyes sharpen-
ing, the Sheriff said, "Maybe that's how you wanted it?"

Rising, tucking away the little case, Wade offered no
response. The Sheriff said, "I see. A man in it, natch'ly.
By advertising yourself, you figure he'll break cover when
you strike close. Don't go yet!"

There was a settled authority in the Sheriff's tone.
Wade found he could accept it without resentment, so he
turned back from the door. Stuart offered him a cigar.

"Look, Forrest. The girl's not here. No guarantee the
man ain't, though. I want you to know that a killing over
a girl ain't classed as justified in my book. *Sabe?*"

"It's fair warning."

"It's meant so." Stuart fired a match for Wade's cigar.
While holding it, he studied Wade. A good man gone
tough, most likely from need rather than choice. Tall,
somewhat too lean for his amount of frame and bone.
His eyes had a remote look in them, like that of long-
unsatisfied hunger. A hard case, this, driven by something
in him that probably would never give him peace as long
as he lived. The Sheriff sighed and said, "I've seen a lot of
trouble over women. Too many wasn't worth it. Go get

drunk, man, an' hit the houses. My own recipe when I was young."

A girl put her head in at the door and called, "Meat pie tonight with—" then stopped, looking at Wade. The Sheriff shifted on his chair so she could see him, and she finished primly, "dumplings."

"Sounds good," Wade commented. He asked the Sheriff, "Any idea where I could eat like that? I'm a stranger here." This caused the girl to bring her gaze back to him in a rapid scrutiny that ended with a smile and nod to the Sheriff.

Following a pause, Stuart said shortly, "Catherine, this is Wade Forrest." He waited for that name to sink in, and bent an expressionless face to Wade. "Miss Larmor, she runs a fine boarding house over on East Street. I eat there sometimes. Yes, Catherine, count me in tonight, please."

"Got room for me?" Wade asked her.

"You mean at the table?"

He thought of back-room number nine. "Both. Room and board. Just for a few days, Miss Larmor."

The Sheriff puffed quickly at his cigar, catching her eye. Wade detected the slight, warning shake of his head. She frowned fleetingly, then told Wade there was room. He thanked her, and she nodded and left: a fair-haired girl rather above medium height, with a firm figure and a straight back. A friendly girl. He thought of that foremost. Friendly. He had not known that candid warmth for some time.

"East Street," the Sheriff said to Wade, "is the one over there on the east side of the town. On this side it's West Street. Like this is West Block and over there it's East Block. Somebody tore loose a lot of imagination on that. It's the only white two-floor house on the street."

He was talking to detain Wade, to keep him from catching up with Catherine Larmor and being seen with her by the gossips. Wade knew it and let him have his way.

"It's a nice house. Respectable. She's a fine girl. I knew her folks. Her father built that house. Died of diphtheria, an' heart trouble got her mother. Went just like that. I try to keep an eye out for Catherine when she ain't looking. She's got a cook there, black gal, and I wouldn't bet on any man's chance if he was to try anything on her. On Catherine, I mean, not the cook. Her name's Katey. Big as Samson. Funny how their names go alike, eh? Catherine an' Katey."

"Yeah, funny. Sheriff, I'm on the hunt for a particular girl—the one I showed you in the picture. Not just any girl. That satisfy you?"

"Well, maybe. Care to tell me who the man is?"

Wade shook his head. "That's what I've got to find out. I have a feeling he's here." He said it sparely, for whatever good it might do toward flushing up his man, and left.

New faces had joined the gathering on the hotel gallery, and men lined the boardwalk below, leaning against the gallery floor and railing. Their bland scanning took in Wade as an object of humorous speculation and muttered jokes. Impossible as it was for him to quench his angry revolt, he held it down, reminding himself not to get graveled at a situation that he had brought purposely on himself.

He canceled his room, got his bag from the clerk and carried it outside. Again the hush closed in around him. Then, as his boot heels rapped the steps to the boardwalk, somebody on the gallery said mockingly, just above a murmur, "Small, dark and pretty. Where, oh, where is she gone?" And that was too much.

Wade set his bag down on the boardwalk and stepped back onto the gallery. "Somebody speak to me?" he inquired, but he spotted his man as he asked.

All faces but one wore fading grins. This one stared steadily at him in a measuring, intent manner. A well-clothed cattleman: good boots, good Stetson. The face had a hard handsomeness. A brittle face, with boldly impulsive eyes. Wade said, "You?"

"I spoke"—The dark, fiery face didn't change, but a force rushed into the eyes and gradually receded—"but not to you."

This could be the man, breaking cover. Wade said, "It better not be to me."

The man lunged. Another man grabbed him and held his arms and whispered to him urgently. Wade shot a glance at the new man. He saw a brown-mottled face and milky blue eyes. Then all the group on the gallery folded around the struggling man, who called furiously from among them, "I'll see you!"

It was halted for now, leaving a bad thing that would have to be settled if he stayed in Maya. Wade said, "I'll be in town a while. My name's Forrest."

"I'm Arne Bassett. I'll be seeing you."

"All right."

He lifted his bag and turned left, passing Toland's Bar next door and the adjoining dance hall on the corner. He turned left again into East Street. Maybe, he thought pinchedly, Arne Bassett was his man. Probably not, though. The world was full of violent hotheads who pushed a joke beyond sensible limits and flared up when it backfired. Arne Bassett had that kind of unreasonable presumption. It showed on his face. But then, too, a man of little boldness would hardly carry off a woman.

He considered the evil of never knowing, of never finding her. By now she could be far down in Mexico, with or without the man. He wiped that picture from his mind, coming abreast of the two-floor white house. He mounted to the porch and knocked on the door. Flowering geraniums in white boxes on the porch sent his thoughts to another house he had always entered with prudent care, worried by fragile knickknacks lurking in wait for an unguarded gesture. He sighed.

He was using his hat to slap dust from his boots, and didn't know the door had opened until Catherine Larmor said softly, laughing, "Save your hat and come in, Mr. Forrest."

She wore an apron over her house dress and her sleeves were rolled back. Her fair hair was done up in thick braids, for convenience he supposed, yet it suited her. There was humor in her hazel eyes, and a frank, unaffected interest. A friendly girl, he thought again, and was glad he had come. This would be a comfortably easygoing house in spite of the geraniums.

But, with his perceptions honed keen, he felt a restraint in her. The Sheriff had spoken his name and made known his disapproval, and she knew about him. Perhaps she was privately reconsidering her decision to take him in. He couldn't blame her. He hadn't had a chance to shave in two days. His shirt and Levis were a month from the wash.

She showed him up to his room, a clean and pleasant one on the cool north side. He was bone tired. He had four hours to go before supper, and the bed called to him. Some remark was in order, though, about the room. He nodded toward the blue curtains at the window and said stupidly, "My wife would like those. She likes blue. Color of her eyes."

Regretting the slip, he went woodenly through the act of thanking Catherine Larmor for her crisp hope that he would be comfortable. She was remembering, of course, that the girl he hunted was dark, not with eyes of light blue. When she had gone he tugged his boots off and lay on the bed. He wearily fended off a bleak despair that was years old, and fell asleep while thinking ironically of Sheriff Stuart's warning.

Katey brought him up his supper, announcing in surprisingly meticulous English that Miss Catherine thought he would prefer to be served in his room this first day. "Meat pie and dumplings, Mr. Forrest. Apple cobbler for after. Coffee, sugar and cream, here. Would you like anything else?" Katey was immense and chocolate brown. Her manner matched his for quiet reserve.

Miss Catherine, he decided, was certainly right. He hadn't washed or shaved or changed clothes. She must have known he'd be too tired and would sleep right to supper time. And Sheriff Stuart would be at the table downstairs.

He was famished. The smell of the good food drew his nose and mouth in to gaunt bareness. "You're Katey?" he took time to say. "I'm glad to know you." His eyes widened on the food.

"I'm glad to know *you*, Mr. Forrest." Katey watched his face.

"Wade."

"Yes, sir, Mr. Wade."

"No. Just Wade, if I'm to call you Katey."

Katey's fine dark eyes regarded him, looking him over, appraising him. Katey smiled a slow, rich smile, passing him her careful approval. "I'll remember. If you want anything, bang on the floor. Any time. The kitchen's right under here."

After supper he shaved, changed clothes, and walked the town while there was still some daylight left. The hub of Maya centered around the East-West Street crossing. On the east side of the main street, coming from the north, you passed shacks, then better houses, Harrison's Emporium, an alley, and the hotel, bar, and dance hall. On the opposite corner of East Street began the row of East Block's neat shops, crowned with a high false-front. This took in the best part of town. Toland's was respectable, catering to ranchers, businessmen and the stage line trade.

The west side was something else: Wright's Livery and a hay-and-grain shed, a saddle-and-harness shop, and a ragged fringe of shacks. West Street was the Mexican section, spilling into the disreputable conglomeration of West Block where the Sheriff's office stood as the one note of respectability. The main street, apparently never named, was simply a bulge in the old Miles Trail, which had become the stage road north and south between Arco and Ute City. Maya was the midway town, set in the heart of Principe Valley.

A voice hailed Wade as he cruised West Block: "Say, the dance hall opens in 'bout half an hour."

He swung around and stood still, instantly attentive to the man who spoke from the doorway of one of the dingy little saloons. A small man, this, wearing close-fitting clothes, a big silver belt-buckle, and silver studs in his leather hatband.

"So? Who're you?"

The man grinned. "I'm Pace. That's Spanish where I come from—California—and called *pahssay*. Here it's Pace, mostly. At that I'm fortunate. It could've been Gutierrajamillo."

"It could. What about the dance hall?"

"Girl there. Small, dark, pretty . . . no, this is no *burla*, man! Pepitte Martin. Ask anybody 'bout Peppy. If she ain't your girl, maybe she can tell you where to look. She gets around. Easy to meet but square. *Discreta. Sabe?*"

"*Sabe.* Thanks."

"*Por nada.* Drink?" Pace shouldered into the saloon, and Wade followed him in and stood the round. The place was a boars' nest but the liquor wasn't too bad: Mexican tequila with a lacing of corn whiskey. It cremated the palate but didn't outrage the stomach. Wade took three drinks with Pace, bought the fat woman-bar-tender a mug of wine, and used up half an hour. Then with a nod to Pace, he left.

The dance hall windows gave out light, but the night was yet too early for the crowd. At the square piano a woman in a red dress plunked and husked a weepy ballad to the almost empty room, while the fiddler drank beer. Wade crossed through into the barroom and bought a drink. He looked around for a place to sit and noticed Pace coming in from the street entrance. It was his guess that Pace had followed him up for more free drinks, and he barely responded to the little Californian's cheery wave. He'd had enough of Pace's chatter.

Every place to the left of the front door was filled. The only table not in use was a big one on the right, near the inside entrance to the dance hall. Unlike the common run of barroom furniture, this was of polished oak. It had carved legs. A fine Navajo blanket draped it. The chairs shoved under it had padded leather seats. He took a step toward it.

Pace laid a hand lightly on his arm. "No, *amigo*, not for us. That's the Tarey table. Rule of the house."

"What?" Wade pulled his arm away. Pace dropped his hand and the amiable grin dimmed. Wade said, "Tarey?"

Pace murmured dryly, "T Anchor. You must be from way off, friend, not to know about T Anchor."

"Not that far."

Having finished his drink standing, Wade raised two fingers to a bartender. Pace saw and grinned amiably again.

"Didn't old Simon Tarey die a few years back, Pace?"

"Right, *señor*. Now it's Miss Beth Tarey, his daughter. It's Tarey everything, here. T Anchor sees to that."

"Even a special table? In a saloon?"

"For old Simon, when he lived," Pace explained. "With the compliments of Toland—who knows how to stand in with the right company. Toland knows better'n to change it, too. He'd have T Anchor down on him. And Deac Shanter. You've heard of him, I guess?"

"We all used to, years ago. Met him once, in Tucson. He shot a monte dealer in the arm and picked up the stakes. Never said a word. Nor anybody else, come to think of it."

"You'll see him again tonight. At that table." Pace was getting a little drunk. He lapsed frequently into dog-Spanish but Wade understood him; he had spent years on the border and in Old Mexico, before going north for what he thought was good reason.

"That old pirate—Simon!" Pace said. He laughed loosely. "He believed in picking a hard crew an' taking what he wanted. Y'know, everybody looked for T Anchor to break up, when he was gone. He was a sea captain 'fore he got in cattle. That's why the anchor brand. Miss Beth was off abroad, Paris or some place. Nobody to take hold. But before he died, old Simon hired Deac Shanter. Son of a gun! He'll be here, Deac Shanter will. An' her. The Tarey, Princess o' Principe."

"How do you know?"

"Toland's wearing his diamond studs, ain't he? An' he's put on two extra floormen from the day crew. An' I heard somebody say he'd got word from Shanter. It was Arne Bassett, come to think."

"Is he here? Where?"

"Oh, he's around," replied Pace vaguely. He drifted off to the door leading into the hotel lobby. Wade saw him speak to a man there, who, when he shifted to sight Wade through the crowd, showed a brown-mottled face and pale blue eyes. Then both men went on into the lobby.

Gone to tip Bassett, Wade thought shortly, and dour disgust for the easy treachery of the drink-cadging Pace plucked at his ready temper. If Bassett was here looking for him, he didn't need any help finding him. If fight was still on Bassett's mind, he'd had plenty of time already to uncork. No, Bassett must have decided to let his threat die. He hadn't the appearance of a patient man who waited for opportunity.

Spending no further thought on that matter, Wade took another look into the dance hall. The woman pianist and the fiddler were at work and some desultory dancing was going on, but only a couple of Mexican girls there answered the description of small, dark, and pretty.

Returning to the barroom, he bought a full bottle, hoping to lighten his gray mood. The old despair was catching up with him, brought on by the laughter and music and girls' swirling skirts. He hauled in a passing floorman by his apron strings, clinked two dollars, and suggested that a chair might be dug up from somewhere.

"Why, sure, colonel!" said the floorman.

"Gracias, mi general!"

Drink, he reflected, sharing a table with three silent cattlemen, was less than a solution for him. Something in him failed to respond to it when he needed it most. Complete and constant drunkenness, he supposed, could help. Blot out all thought, memory, everything. But a drunkard was pitiful. He was not yet unable to bear his burden.

The three cattlemen at the table were cronies. They had spared grudging nods when he asked for space. They weren't playing cards and there was room for half a dozen. They didn't speak to him so he didn't offer his bottle. Friends of Arne Bassett, he guessed. To hell with them. He kept an eye out for Pepitte Martin. Some of the dance hall girls were coming into the barroom now, with their men partners. A tab for the girl went with every drink. Turn-in value, twenty cents. Well, hell, the girls had to live.

The front door banged open. A man's voice called out strongly, "All right, George!"

When a floorman hurriedly whisked the Navajo blanket off the big table, Wade knew he was about to witness a Tarey entrance. It was, he conceded, a grand dilly of an entrance; nothing like it since Maximilian entered Mexico City with his Hapsburg band.

The floor between the door and the table cleared quickly. The noise in the adjoining dance hall quieted. The music stopped. Silence spread even to the poker tables and halted the flicking slap of cards, murmured calls, click of chips. Toland ducked out from behind the bar, diamond studs glittering in his white linen shirt, motioning curtly to a floorman to help the first one slide out the Tarey padded leather chairs.

Arne Bassett strode in from the hotel lobby, smiling, to stand at the head of the long oak table. He laid both hands on the back of the chair there.

A man entered, a brown-eyed, brown-haired man with a square face heavied by a full jaw and wide flat lips. A supreme self-assurance, close to arrogance, carried his straight stare to Bassett, to the table, to Toland. "All right, George?"

"Yes, Mr. Brouk."

Arne Bassett took his hands off the back of the chair and stepped away. His face changed. He had the look now that Wade had seen on the hotel gallery—the look of violence held in uncertain leash, but sharper and more naked. Wade knew then that Bassett's mind had been occupied tonight by something more pressing than a stranger's challenge.

The brown man, Brouk, ignored Bassett. He· said, "Okay, George."

"Let, then," Wade thought satirically, "the party commence. Bow down. The royal Tarey comes!" He took another drink from his bottle, clinking it noisily to the glass.

The woman came in then on the arm of a tall man. He had expected to see a weather-beaten, mannish female who would flourish a jeweled hand and order drinks for the house. Instead he found himself staring at a woman who could, truly and without hedging, be called beautiful. A full-blooming woman of perhaps thirty, endowed with the glory of jade-green eyes and chestnut hair and a flawless skin, white at the throat, smooth as cream. She wore a maroon dress, its tight bodice manifesting her awareness of her figure. No shy modesty encumbered her. Her movements were sure, leisurely. Her green eyes sparkled a gay unconcern for her surroundings. She had the nonchalance of one who was at home anywhere and knew no need to follow rules of niggling sedateness.

The dance hall girls, hushed and watching, were drab by contrast, cheaply ordinary in finery that a moment ago had given color to the barroom.

Wade recognized the tall man beside her as Deac Shanter. Now as in Tucson the veteran gunfighter wore a gravely ministerial air enhanced by his black knee-length coat, black tie and plain black riding boots. But the slightly rakish slant of his wide-brimmed hat suggested a leaning of saint toward sinner, and the face under it added strongly to that impression. Deac Shanter's face bannered ruthless strength at the muscled brows, a predatory quality in the beaked line of his nose, and the sardonic humor of a satyr in the wide, hard mouth. His deep-set gray eyes contained an inhuman calmness and nothing else.

Chewing on a long cigar, Deac Shanter escorted Beth Tarey with casual courtesy to the head of the table and took the chair on her left. Brouk seated himself on her right.

There were no others in their party until Beth Tarey spoke to Shanter, who bent his head to her, listened, then leaned back without a word or nod. In a moment Shanter glanced around at Arne Bassett and pointed his cigar at a chair. Bassett took that chair, bowing first to Beth Tarey, who smiled and gave him her hand. Brouk didn't look at him.

To one after another of men in the barroom Shanter sent the same unspoken invitation, never declined. The blank glance. The pointing cigar. He was the impassive *major-domo* executing the wishes of the ruling queen.

The table began filling up, while the hush over the barroom grew painful. Beth Tarey murmured to Shanter again. He drew a gold case from his coat pocket and snapped it open. She chose a cigarette from it and he struck and held a match for her.

Wade admired that. A woman was rare and outstanding who could hold Deac Shanter in line. Shanter was masterless, never tamed, a man of tall reputation. The tales once related about him were rich in crackling comedy of a tough and often bizarre type. He had stretched personal independence and roughshod enterprise far beyond the law's limits, then faced about and made it stick. Having no nerves and a full share of brains, he was as dangerous a gambler as he was a gunfighter. He had always been a lone wolf, playing his cards for their full value to himself; win all or lose all. Yet he had an eccentric streak, quixotic and unpredictable. Within the space of five minutes he could be coldly savage and magnificently generous. Mexican *pobres* adored him and had sheltered him when his fortunes were low and the posses were out.

The blank glance found Wade. It came as a shock to meet those utterly calm and compelling gray eyes. Wade sat still. Deac Shanter made a motion to him, a brief circling of long fingers holding the cigar. Wade rose. He remembered his bottle and picked it up. The three cattlemen at his table stared. He carried the bottle with him.

"My name's Forrest," he said to Shanter. "We met once. In Tucson."

"I remember." Like his eyes, Shanter's voice completely lacked emotion of any kind. "The Southern Star." Rising, he dipped his cigar at his own chair. "Sit down." He shifted over to the next empty chair, and Wade sat down next to Beth Tarey.

Wade clunked his bottle on the table. He was riled by his own obedience to the curt summons. Out of the mischief of raddled temper he asked Beth Tarey, "Drink?"

It was enough to get him in trouble. You said that, in that offhand way, to a dance hall girl. The men at the table straightened. All but Deac Shanter. He chewed on his cigar, looking at nothing.

Beth Tarey raised her brows, as if more surprised than offended. Then she smiled a humorous understanding smile, recognizing his rudeness as a deliberate incivility aimed at the company rather than at herself. Wade's unbrushed hair, dark on top, reddish over the ears, gave him a rough and shaggy appearance. That which stirred the indrawn remoteness of his eyes was anger. Anger at the imperious summons, his compliance, and the stiff disdain of Arne Bassett and the rest.

Beth Tarey said over her shoulder to the hovering Toland, "George—glasses, please."

Her jade eyes met Wade's levelly. He discovered more than humor in her gaze and he deepened his mask of guarded control. This woman was dangerous. Most likely she enjoyed the game of bringing together men who were at odds, to observe results and exercise her dominance over them. He sat there waiting.

"You and Deac seem to have met before," she said. "As you may know, Deac is manager of T Anchor."

Wade nodded. Shanter lifted his cigar in casual acknowledgment while surveying the crowded barroom.

"And I think—" Beth Tarey's voice and eyes evinced amused knowledge—"you've met Mr. Bassett. He's a neighbor of ours. Gunsight Ranch."

Arne Bassett stared dead-on at Wade and offered no sort of greeting. Wade merely stared back.

"Mr. Brouk. Also a neighbor. Frank has the Bar V."

Frank Brouk ran his brown eyes over Wade contemptuously, nodded, and looked away.

The rest were ranch owners, too. Small, Wade guessed, compared to Tarey and Bassett and Brouk. They held inferior levels in the Principe hierarchy, allowing them the privilege to sit at the Tarey table. From a long experience of such patterns he sensed the usual conflict among them. They sat in cliques and there was no general exchange of talk. A cloud of enmities overhung this table, with the mutual hatred of Arne Bassett and Frank Brouk at the black core. It was as obvious as the division cutting fraternal ties on election day.

There wasn't enough in Wade's bottle to go around. Toland himself brought fresh bottles and filled the glasses. Two floormen hurried with water fetched from the cooler. Beth Tarey picked up her glass and gazed down the table, her eyes halting at each man. She sipped. Their glasses rose. She sent a faint smile at Deac Shanter, as if in triumph. Shanter swallowed his drink and looked blandly back at her for an instant.

She bent toward Wade. "You're a new man here."

"Yes."

She smiled at him. "Take it easy. You make enemies too fast."

"I seem to around here."

"Are you staying?"

"For a while."

She studied him appreciatively. His was a blunt-boned face, brown, as impassive as Shanter's, yet having a mobile quality like that of muscle under tight-fitted buckskin. She spoke across him to Shanter. "Can we use him at T Anchor?"

Without removing his eyes from the crowd Shanter said dryly, "Sure. Rep rider. See me tomorrow, Forrest."

"I'll think it over," Wade said, meaning to hell with it. He spotted a girl in a green dress stepping in from the dance hall. A small girl, dark-haired, perhaps pretty. Her back was toward him.

"Excuse," he murmured to Beth Tarey, and shoved his chair back and got up. The girl happened to turn, but he couldn't see her face clearly in the smoke of the barroom. He went to her.

The men at the table followed him with their eyes. Deac Shanter sent a ghost of a smile at Beth Tarey, who gazed steadily at her fingernails. At that moment Beth Tarey was for once a rejected woman, and Shanter said softly to her, "He's no good, lady." She flicked him a look of dislike and he ranged his glance off over the crowd again, chewing his cigar.

The dark little girl smiled uncertainly at Wade as he came up, but when he stopped before her she rounded her eyes in mock consternation, moving so that he shielded her from view of the Tarey table.

"Mister, you've just made a certain lady despise me for all petrified eternity." She chuckled. "By morning everybody'll be saying how a man dropped her for little Peppy Martin. Oh, sweet Maria!"

Her face was not that of the girl in the picture. She was pretty, a likable gamin with a grin and a few faint freckles on her short nose. "Hello, Peppy," he said, looking around for chairs. "My name's Wade."

"Glad to know you." She slipped a hand through his arm and walked with him to the table where the three cattlemen still sat. "How 'bout it, boys?" she inquired of them cheerfully. They rose surlily and left. Wade seated her and took the chair facing her.

"Champagne?"

"You have to buy the whole bottle. Twelve dollars." She shook her head. "I wouldn't stick you for that. You don't look rich." Her glance flitted impudently to the Tarey table and back to him. "Port. It's more ladylike than whiskey."

He bought it at the bar, and a whiskey for himself. They touched glasses. She set the port aside after a bare sip. She laced her fingers under her chin, elbows on the table.

"Wade, what are you up to?"

"Hunting a lost girl. She's small, dark, and pretty. Any suggestions?"

"Well, there's me. Only I'm not lost."

He produced the gutta-percha case, opened it, and slid it over the table to her. "Any other suggestions?"

She frowned thoughtfully down at the picture without taking it up. "Now, where've I seen somebody like her?" she muttered, and Wade leaned forward, watching for a false overplay, a string-along.

Pace and the mottled-faced man entered from the hotel lobby. They came up directly behind Peppy's chair. Pace passed on by to stand near the front door, but his companion loitered, looking down at the girl. "Peppy," he said, "I'll buy you a drink."

She nodded absently, then turned her head.

"Well, Mr. Perse! I never would've believed you'd offer a duck a drink if you owned a lake. Sweet Maria, what else can happen to me tonight?"

She winked at Wade and put her attention back on the picture. "I remember now. Could've been her. She'd been crying, I could see. Eyes all red. Would that be so?"

"That," Wade said very quietly, "could be so."

Perse, still behind Peppy, reached out over her to pick up the picture. Wade slapped his hand on it, staring up stonily at him, and drew it in to his side of the table. He closed the case and put it away. "You could get your fingers burned that way," he remarked.

"Could I?" Dragging out the empty chair beside Peppy, Perse seated himself on its edge. His pale eyes regarded her fixedly.

As though suddenly conscious of time running short, Peppy said to Wade, "Three men were with her. Two riding ahead, the other driving a buggy with her in it beside him. The two riders wore slickers. It was starting to rain. I couldn't tell what they looked like, from the back, in those slickers and their hats pulled down. But the other one, the one driving the buggy—"

"A talky female is sure tiresome," Perse broke in.

Wade laid a look on him and said, "I'd leave, was I you. Go on, Peppy. What was he like?"

"He had white hair and a red face. Thin. Wore some kind of Indian shirt. The girl turned her face to me as I crossed past, like she had half a mind to speak, but I was in a hurry. It was way west of town, and I had a livery horse out and no slicker, and so I didn't—"

Perse pushed his hand against Peppy's mouth. "Shut up," he said.

Wade reached over the table, hit Perse full in the mouth with the heel of his palm, and stood up, watching fury flood into the mottled face.

"I told you," he murmured.

For a moment Perse sat back, fingers to his bruised lips. Then he leaped around the table and came swinging at Wade.

At the Tarey table Beth spoke to Bassett. "Some of your work, Arne?"

"Oh, no, Beth," he protested. "I—"

"Liar," she said coolly. "Watch it, Deac."

Deac Shanter nodded, and his glance stopped Toland. Frank Brouk sent an oblique look at Beth, cupped his square face in his hands and frowningly watched the fight.

Wade stepped wide away from the table and slashed his right fist into Perse's middle. Perse grunted and came on. hooking at Wade and landing one. His rushing momentum carried him past so that he kicked into Wade's vacated chair and all but took a header over it. He legged the chair away, cursing, whirling around, regaining his balance.

Wade rubbed his neck where Perse had hit him and waited for Perse's next bulling rush. He had a momentary sight of the barroom, an impression of everybody standing except those at the Tarey table. Perse charged. Wade ducked in and struck twice before Perse elbowed him into the empty table. It crashed and Wade toppled headlong over it. Perse followed him around, and kicked.

He rolled fast. Perse's boot heel scraped his cheek and somebody among the onlookers uttered a loud, "Arrgh!" of disgust.

Wade bounded up and tore in for a kill. It was savage and pitiless. He shook off a blow above his eyes and drove a straight left into Perse's face. He followed it up with a right. Perse's head snapped back. Wade repeated. Perse sagged, gasping, clawing at him. Wade kneed him off, took deliberate stance, and struck brutally hard, a down-driving, hammering smash. He felt a crunch under his knuckles and the impact ran up his arm.

Perse sprawled heavily on the floor with the sound of a dropped sack of bones. He lay sobbing harshly, done, and Wade moved slowly away from him, breathing hard.

Beth Tarey said to Bassett, "It didn't work out for you, Arne. Better try it yourself next time." She smiled, watching Wade stand spread-legged, his stare searching the crowd for Pace, for signs of anybody who might want a follow-up fight.

"Deac, he's a good man. Hire him."

Shanter sent an imperative, dismissing gesture to Toland. If Beth wanted the man, he was hired.

Two floormen lifted Perse, as efficiently as if he were just another drunk, and bore him across the barroom into the hotel. At a sign from Toland another bustled out to fetch the doctor. Arne Bassett kept twirling his glass on the Tarey table. He would not look up from it, although many eyes scanned him questioningly, for Perse was his man. Frank Brouk retired massively into a cloak of disinterest.

Toland brought Wade two inches of whiskey in a tumbler. Wade drank some and used the remainder to bathe his cut knuckles. As he tramped by the Tarey table to the front door, Deac Shanter said to him, "See me tomorrow."

"I'll think it over," he answered as before.

Outside, he turned into East Street, nursing his knuckles and reflecting that he must talk further with Peppy Martin. He heard a man round the corner after him. He swung about and made out the baggily ungraceful shape of Sheriff Stuart.

The Sheriff advanced into the light of the dance hall's side windows, hands in his trouser pockets and round hat on the back of his head. His pudgy face expressed tired disapproval.

"Yeah," Wade told him, "I had a little trouble in Toland's. Nothing serious. It shouldn't concern you."

Shifting out of the direct light, Stuart dug a dead cigar stump from his cheap holder. "Doesn't concern me so far," he agreed mildly. "Could later, though. You sure would save me trouble if you drifted on, Forrest. Your girl ain't here."

"I got reason tonight to think she might be."

Stuart sighed. "Can't you find another? You don't appear to meet too much obstacle in that direction." The comment was a dry one, containing tolerant sarcasm without envy.

"She's the one I'm out to find," Wade said, and walked on up East Street.

"You turning in?" Stuart called after him.

"Yeah."

"G'night, Forrest."

Katey met him in the hall after he closed the front door and started for the stairs. She glimpsed his face under the hall lamp and exclaimed softly, "Oh, my!" He grinned ruefully and went up the stairs to his room, glad it hadn't been Catherine Larmor who saw him come home in that state.

Soon Katey knocked and came into his room, bringing fresh towels and a pitcher of water. "Wet these and lay them on," she told him. "They'll hold the swelling down. Here's a letter the hotel clerk sent over. Looks like it's followed you all over everywhere. Wait, I'll light your lamp."

"Thanks, Katey."

"Coffee coming."

He opened the letter, noting its nearly month-old date. Reading it under the light, he got half through, sat down slowly on the edge of the bed, and began again at the first line. Then he read right through.

Katey brought hot coffee. He raised his eyes from the letter and stared blindly at her. Confronted by the horror ravaging his grayed face, she whispered, "Man, dear, what's wrong with you?"

He swallowed and shook his head. Heaving to his feet, he stumbled past Katey out of the room, down the stairs, out of the house. He left his hat and gun behind on the bed. In the street he let his fingers open, dropping the crumpled letter, heedlessly letting the night breeze bowl it away in the dust.

"Whiskey," he said to the fat woman in the dirty little saloon on West Block.

At some time during the night Peppy Martin shook his shoulder and sank hurriedly into the chair across the table from him. "Wade, quit drinking and get out of here. You won't find her."

He considered for a minute, having difficulty holding his head up, his hands spread on the table. "Not looking for her any more," he managed. "Finished."

"Good. Listen, Wade, I've got to go. I'm taking the night stage. Come along with me."

His left hand forgot its job and let him down. His head bumped the table and he sighed deeply and closed his eyes.

"Wade, come along! Josefita, give me a hand with him. Damn you, you fat sow—"

The fat woman mumbled something scaredly in Spanish.

A man called gently from the street, "Now, Peppy. Be a good girl, hear? We're holdin' the stage for you."

After that it was silent. Wade slept until some men came and dragged him out.

CHAPTER 2

CATHERINE LARMOR's boarding house was a well-lived-in home. Her boarders, mostly unattached and middle-aged men employed in or near town, called it their home and in spare time took care of such painting and small repair tasks as required masculine skills. Still, going downstairs from his room, Wade felt self-conscious. His own room had become very familiar to him, but the lower part of the house was unknown territory.

At the foot of the stairs he paused, tempted to go on out, but restrained by the ungraciousness of such an act after all that had happened. Frowning at his momentary weakness, he walked along the carpeted hall and looked through an open doorway into what was evidently the dining room. He entered, stalking kitchen noises.

Katey, coming in from another door with a stack of plates, greeted him with a warm, "Well, hello!" and scanned his face.

"Hello, Katey."

Catherine Larmor appeared at the door behind Katey. Wade saw that she, too, couldn't restrain a searching look at his face. It had taken him better than half an hour to shave, but he had done the job fairly well.

"Hello."

This, he thought, must be what it was like for a man, dressed and restored to masculine dignity, when he met the nurse who had known him at his sick, helpless worst. If the nurse were plain and elderly, that made it easier. But Catherine Larmor was as feminine as a fresh young housewife, dusting flour from her hands, causing any man to have pensive thoughts about her.

"I want to thank you," he said soberly.

She made a small, deprecating wing-flick with her hands.

"We take that for granted. We only hope you'll be all right now."

He stood groping for something that he had intended to bring up. Not finding it, and growing embarrassed at the lengthening pause, he said, "I'm going out for a while. Anyhow, thanks again."

He got to the front door and had it open, when he recollected. Closing the door, he started back along the carpeted hall. But he stopped before reaching the dining room, overhearing Katey comment, "He's a man, he ever cut loose!" She spoke in a normal tone, thinking him out of the house, and Wade began a stealthy retreat, not wishing to embarrass her.

"Married to one woman and chasing another!" retorted Catherine. "Drinking with Beth Tarey and getting into a saloon brawl over Peppy Martin! What do you call that?"

"He's a lonesome man. He's got sad, hungry eyes."

"They often have, his kind. Katey, you're a fool."

"I guess I've got lots of company, Miss Catherine."

"Pooh! Let's get the roast in the oven."

Wade waited until kitchen noises started up again. He eased the front door open and shut it soundlessly behind him. He crossed the porch with its white-potted plants and descended to the street. The late morning sun blazed on him, its outdoor warmth familiar and good. His right hand plucked at his empty shirt pocket and he thought drearily of the small, dark, pretty girl. His shirt was freshly washed and ironed. Katey had done that, he supposed. Katey, the only one in Maya who still thought well of him. It would be all over town, of course, about what had happened.

From the dance hall corner he angled across the main street toward West Block. This weekday, no traffic kicked up dust. He felt conspicuous—a puncher not at work in roundup season.

Sheriff Stuart loafed to the door of his office under the faded sign and stood leaning there, waiting for him. As Wade drew close the Sheriff asked amiably, "How's it goin'?"

"Better than it might've been."

Neither of them spoke for a spell, watching a burro

plod out from the alley alongside Harrison's. The burro stretched its neck, brayed into the quiet street, and solemnly plodded back.

"Does it this time every day," Stuart commented. "You can set your watch by him." He dipped a glance at the small gold watch that Wade fished absently from a trouser pocket. "I see you still got one."

"It was in my bag, in my room."

"Lucky. Like a drink?"

"With you, yes." Wade followed him into the office and Stuart produced a bottle and two glasses from his desk. Watching him pour the drinks, Wade recalled the pudgy face bent over him, and the surprisingly gentle hands. He started to speak of it, but Stuart looked up and asked, "That enough?"

"Plenty. Don't worry, it won't set me off on another soak. That one about did me up."

"Doc Meek says it was more than that."

Wade felt the scars on his face. "He should know. He took the bandages off this morning."

"More than that. Before that happened."

"Knockout drops?" Wade raised his glass. "To you," he said, and drank. "Doc could be right. I never was out like that before. Did Josefita do it to me?"

Stuart rolled a shoulder. "She's skipped. Visiting her folks somewhere."

"Tell me just what happened."

"You could get it from Catherine Larmor. Or Katey."

"I know. But I'm asking you, sir."

" 'Sir'?" The Sheriff put his glass down.

"A form of respect," Wade murmured. "No *burla*."

"Thank you." Stuart took his glass up and politely bobbed his round, bald head. "All right. You went on a high lonesome, after you told me you were turning in. That was Sa'day night. Sunday morning, 'bout four, I found you down the end of West Street in some weeds. Somebody'd done a job on you. Boots and what-all. Your face—well, I only knew you by your shirt. The back, that is. Front was all blood. You sure were a mess. That was Sunday 'fore last."

"Nine days ago," Wade said. He could recall fragments of the first two days, maybe three, in his room. He remembered Catherine and Katey whispering as they attended to him. "Well?"

"I lugged you here. Catherine came for you later, when she heard." The Sheriff wagged his cigar holder. "She's done it before. Her boarders are her folks, so don't build any special ideas on it. Her and Katey an' me drug you to your room an' called Doc Meek. All the church-going folks saw it. Me being there, though, made it halfway legal. How much did you lose?"

"Hundred dollars, more or less." Wade handed back his empty glass, shaking his head to Stuart's nod at the bottle. He said, "They stole that picture. Why?"

Stuart frowned. "It was dark."

"Where does Peppy Martin stay?"

"She's gone. Took the stage south that night. Girls like her, they come an' go."

Wade got his tobacco sack and wheatsheaves and rolled a cigarette carefully, his gaze far away. "I remember," he said. "She told me she had to go. Then it got dark and two men helped me out. I didn't see them." He considered, and then queried, "Know a fellow named Pace? Talky little joker. From California, he says."

"Concho Pace. Gunsight rider."

"That's Bassett's outfit. Perse is Gunsight, too, eh?"

"Gunsight foreman," Stuart admitted. "But you're seein' trail that ain't there. Arne Bassett's got a bronco streak, but he ain't crazy. You hit town with a chip on, an' you told Arne off. Perse, he's Arne's faithful dog, so he braced you that night. But that's only reasonable. It don't signify that Perse worked you over later. I doubt if he could, the shape you put him in. No, you just picked the wrong place, Josefita's. You're not the first."

"That's skinning it down," Wade allowed. "But look. Pace put me on to Peppy Martin. Then he teamed with Perse and they came to our table. I figured they were out to brace me for Bassett. It did happen that Peppy had something to tell me when I showed her the picture, so I sat tight. Before Pace had time to get set, Perse pushed the play. Peppy was talking too much to suit him."

He watched for a break in Stuart's disbelieving expression, but the Sheriff only asked curiously, "What set you off on that high lonesome, anyhow?"

Wade looked out into the sun-glared street. In a mo-

ment he said, "Later that night two unknown jiggers—
maybe more—get me off in the dark and beat hell out of
me. They rob me down to my last cent and take that
picture. If it was just robbery, they didn't need to half-
kill me. I was out. It was meant to warn me to drift—
like Peppy was warned to drift before she could tell me
anything more."

That brought a sour grunt. "You're guessin' wild."

"No. I've had time to recollect some things and put
them in place. Peppy was scared and mad when she tried
to get me out of Josefita's. Somebody told her to get
going. I heard him."

Slumped untidily in his chair, Stuart ran a slow, counting perusal over the checkerboard of wanted bills tacked
on the wall behind Wade. As if that were his usual pre-
liminary to dozing off, he closed his eyes. Wade sat the
silence out, smoking.

At last, without opening his eyes, Stuart spoke.

"Forrest, listen. Bassett's Gunsight range takes in
roughly half of High Folds. That's east of T Anchor.
Frank Brouk's place, Bar V, covers the other half of
High Folds to the south. They both thrived there on the
nod of Simon Tarey, who held all the grass he wanted—
just about all the rest of the South Principe, in fact. T
Anchor could crowd out Gunsight or Bar V any time.
Bassett an' Brouk always played up to Simon, each trying
to get ahead of the other in his good books, in case he ever
got a taste for some o' that High Folds grass."

"That setup doesn't seem to have changed much,"
Wade observed, thinking of the undercurrent of antago-
nisms at the Tarey table in Toland's.

"That's exactly it. I guess they've both asked Beth
Tarey forty times to marry 'em. If she marries one he'll
eat the other. He'll be king. Last year T Anchor fought
a grass blight. This year it's worse. If T Anchor gets to
needing more range, Deac Shanter won't stop a minute at
moving onto High Folds. Lately, Arne Bassett has had
the edge over Brouk with Beth Tarey. Now, d'you begin
to see the powder barrel you're messin' into?"

Wade clumped to his feet, flipping the stub of his
cigarette out through the open door. The Sheriff raised
his eyelids and peered up at him.

"Forrest, I ask you, would Arne Bassett do such a fool

thing as get tangled with some girl now? Would he so much as look at a girl, him courting Beth Tarey an' his whole future in her hands? Use sense!"

Wade watched the dying smoke curl thinly from the stub in the dirt outside. "It's not likely."

"Not likely," Stuart agreed. He yawned and wiped his eyes. "Here's another thing. East beyond High Folds there's Starvation Hills. According to their location, those two-bit Starvation cowmen back either Bassett or Brouk. They know that if either one gets pushed back by T Anchor, he's got to move in on them, on his closest Starvation neighbors. To save his herds, he's got to, if it means fight. It's a case of what-d'you-call-it—self-preservation— all round. With T Anchor on top of the heap. Man, you just whisper a word against Bassett or Brouk, an' you bring a bunch of Starvation cowmen down on your neck. Besides, naturally, Bassett or Brouk." The Sheriff polished his cigar holder on his sleeve. "There it is. I've told you."

The morning was passing and Wade had somewhere to go. He asked, "Who's the thin *hombre* with the white hair, red face and Indian shirt?"

Slightly confused for once, Stuart jolted up to inspect the street. "Max Luttrell in town? He better not be!"

"Why not?"

The street was empty. Stuart fitted a cigar into his holder and lighted it. He lifted a resentful stare at Wade.

"What the hell is this?" he demanded.

"I asked you about Max Luttrell."

"All right. I'll throw Luttrell in jail any chance he gives me. He lives with some Navajos, down Black Walls. He sells 'em whiskey. He's got an Indian squaw. They say he comes of a good family back East. I've never seen much sign of it. Where'd you pick his name up?"

"Thanks, Mr. Stuart," Wade said. "I'll be seeing you."

He entered the white house on East Street and walked along the hall into the dining room. Catherine Larmor and Katey came out of the kitchen and greeted him in two tones: one reserved, the other quietly warm.

"Hello, Mr. Forrest."

"Coffee, Wade?"

"Thanks, I'd like some, Katey."

Catherine raised an eyebrow at Katey's use of the first

name. Katey said tranquilly, "You too, Miss Catherine. We got time. Sit down, both, won't you?"

Wade pulled out chairs and said to Catherine. "I'm taking a job at T Anchor. I've run up a bill here."

"T Anchor credit is good," she informed him levelly.

They sat drinking coffee at one end of the long dining table. He brought out the little gold watch and placed it on the table and said, "Please take this."

She hardly glanced down at it. "No security required."

"Kind of you." He looked around and said, "Katey, I'd like you to have this."

Katey came forward and slowly picked up the watch. It shone in her brown hand. It had an enameled, flowered face. "I bet," she murmured, "you bought it somewhere for your wife. Didn't you? It's a lady's watch."

"Yes," he said gently. "I did. But she's dead now."

They both made some sort of movement, swift and inclining toward him. He kept his eyes on his cup of coffee. His scarred face tightened and he felt a twitch quiver up his cheek and he pressed his fingers against it. "I'd like to tell you," he said. "I think you should know." He looked at Catherine.

Her eyes were the softest he had ever seen. Katey's were somber and drawn, weighted with memories of her own. He said, "I was mavericking in the Big Bend country, combing for strays. My partner got killed. Horse fell on him. I had known him a long time. He supported his sister. She had the *paraliz.* Helpless most of her life. I took her north. He asked me."

He smiled faintly, his eyes gently musing. "It was a small town. They didn't understand, so we got married. She sat in a chair I built. It had wheels."

Catherine lowered her head.

"We got a nice little house. I took jobs, paying jobs. Had to have money for medicine and stuff. The medicine, it was the only way she could sleep."

He lifted his coffee cup, looked closely at it, drank dregs. "That letter. She drank all the medicine, night after I left. She went to sleep and never woke up. That was nearly a month ago."

Putting the cup down, he said, "I've got to see Shanter about that job."

Catherine followed him to the porch and stood with

him in the sun. "Katey will take care of the watch," she told him. "She likes fine things. She worked a long time for three maiden sisters who ran a young ladies' finishing school in Boston." She was talking to bridge a dismal gap, for on his face was growing again the deep, stoic look of personal isolation. Then hurrying, she said, "I hope you'll like the T Anchor job," and her tone held a question founded on her thought of Beth Tarey.

"Rep rider. I've had worse."

He touched his hat to her in a gravely courteous salute and she looked after him until he turned the corner into the main street.

He cut over to Wright's Livery. Jim Wright, hearing his boots on the battered planks of the runway, poked his head out of his tiny office. Wade asked him, "Can I get a nag on credit to ride out to T Anchor? I'm going to work there."

Jim Wright nodded, coming out to him, running a look of inquisitive interest over Wade's face. "Matter fact, Deac Shanter left a T Anchor horse here for you. You'll find him at Glory Spring. That's the home ranch. Shanter's gen'rally there."

Surprise and a slow exasperation washed through Wade and receded. Deac Shanter was coolly taking it for granted that he would accept his offer of a job. That colored the offer with a shade of command. Yet it was difficult to take in bad part the man's thoughtful consideration in leaving him a horse.

Wade asked Wright for directions to Glory Spring. He got them, saddled the T Anchor horse and rode out. He had to pass West Block, and Sheriff Stuart hailed him.

"Driftin' on, Forrest?" Then taking note of the horse and its brand, Stuart aimed a straight stare at him and demanded sharply, "What's this?"

"I work for T Anchor," Wade said.

"After what I've told you?"

"What's that got to do with it?"

Stuart, evidently realizing that he had somewhat stepped over his boundary, pulled a bleakly humorous face. He was steeped in the knowledge of his trade and its limitations. None knew better than he that a law officer in country such as this was expected to keep his authority pared down to its minimum, restrict his duties to un-

avoidable essentials, and step clear of anything that didn't
officially concern him. So all he said was, "You're headin'
for more trouble. More than you or any one man can
handle. Well, it's your affair."

"I'll keep it mine."

Wade took the road south out of Maya onto the old
Miles Trail, a wheel-rutted ribbon running down through
the heart of the South Principe. In half an hour he reached
the west turn-off mentioned by Wright. For a while he
was riding directly toward the mountain range of Los
Freyes; then the trail bent south until he guessed he
traveled about parallel to the Miles. It curved later in
gradually ascending loops, climbing over a long spur of
foothills, and at its highest point he halted to blow his
horse and fix the pattern of the country in his mind.

From up here the immensity of the grassed flats could
be fully recognized. The range stretched in a sheer sweep,
not broken until it piled up into High Folds on the far
eastern side of the valley. He picked out a dot, a rider,
crawling up in the direction where he figured Arne Bassett's Gunsight should be located. Frank Brouk's Bar V
lay somewhere farther south on that side. Starvation Hills,
rising beyond High Folds, appeared crinkled and gray
from here, which meant rock ridges and a hustling for
graze.

This, then—all worth having this side of High Folds—
was T Anchor. A great ranch, well located, prosperous,
powerfully able to reach out and take what it wanted
whenever it wanted it. And, unlike most famed outfits of
its size, not controlled by a syndicate, but owned entirely
by one person, a woman. Simon Tarey had created something big. Beth Tarey was a very rich woman.

Wade tightened cinch and remounted and put his horse
to a walk, and he descended through the timber and
swung west up along a narrow stream of crystal-clear
water. Presently, as he rounded a bulge of huge lichen-
green rock, the land spread out and he approached a
house.

The house was large, built of stone and adobe up to
three feet of foundation, with peeled logs above that, well
chinked. A roofed gallery ran around the two sides visible
to him, and giant cottonwoods and willows nourished by
the stream shaded it. There was a long bunkhouse farther

on, a barn, wagon shed, blacksmith shed, a dugout root cellar and a cooler, and sundry other buildings. This was a real ranch. Even the yard was fenced, and the entrance into it was composed of two twenty-foot upright logs supporting a squared log that blazoned the deeply carved brand of the uncompromisingly plain T and the rounded curves of the Anchor.

He rode under the brand into the yard. The blacksmith could be heard hammering in methodical tempo at something, occasionally bouncing his hammer on the anvil to retain his rhythm during an instant of pondering on where to strike next. Outside of that ringing music of labor the yard lay silent and empty. Wade passed on to the corrals below the bunkhouse. He unsaddled his horse, turned it in and racked the saddle. As he tramped back, Deac Shanter emerged onto the front gallery of the house and stood looking at him.

As in town, Shanter wore his black broadcloth coat, white shirt, four-in-hand tie and wide-brimmed hat. Nobody had ever seen him wearing less. There was about him a coldly dignified indifference, yet the calm power of his gaze struck like a jolting blow. His deep-set gray eyes grasped and dominated what they fastened on. It was as though he held within himself some enormous destructive force, and could afford the luxury of a grim and secret sense of humor.

Wade stepped to the gallery, and Deac Shanter remarked to him, "Doc Meek knows his business."

"Proved it with me," Wade said.

Shanter swung around, giving a beckoning motion, and Wade entered the house. After a hall, the room they went into was sparely furnished with a desk and some shelves. Obviously this was the ranch office. To an elderly man wearing an eyeshade Shanter said, "Forrest. New man. Start him on the payroll beginning Saturday before last."

The elderly bookkeeper glanced up, nodded, scribbled a note. Wade said, "I haven't been working all that time."

They took no notice. Shanter paced out, repeating the beckoning motion—a curt jerk of a thumb—and led him into the main room. It was a room at least forty feet by thirty, furnished in the roughly handsome style of this

Mexican-tinged country: Indian rugs and rawhide chairs, a huge table, *trastero*-fronted cupboards.

Shanter opened a cupboard and placed a bottle and two glasses on the table. He filled a glass for himself first and shoved the bottle to Wade.

A minor ceremony, this, awarded to a new man as a formal welcome. From all accounts T Anchor rarely took on new hands. T Anchor actually was a group of ranches run under the Tarey brand and Shanter's management. By an efficient system it kept its crews steadily employed the year around. Winter lay-offs and hirings the following spring, customary on most ranches, were unknown on T Anchor.

Wade said, "Thanks, I've had a drink today," and inspected the room. The windows were bare, the Indian rugs placed with small regard for decorative arrangement. This was a man's house, everything about it pointing to utility and convenience.

Deac Shanter said dryly, "No, Miss Tarey doesn't live here. She's built a place for herself on the Miles, below Maya, that she's called Los Portales. Miss Tarey likes company. She keeps open house there." He gazed at Wade and his eyes took on a smokiness. "Not for the hands. T Anchor hands don't call at Los Portales unless invited."

Wade said, "Naturally." He knew enough not to build on Beth Tarey's friendliness in Toland's. She had passed the word to hire him, but Shanter was the T Anchor ramrod. "Thanks for leaving me a horse at Wright's," he said, not quite filtering a roughness from his voice.

Deac Shanter's wide, flat lips quirked. "I figured you wouldn't want to drift 'til you find who worked you over. You're broke and in need of a job. Rep rider for T Anchor is no snap, but it'll give you time to circulate around."

Wade met the coldly opaque eyes. Before they blanked completely he thought he discerned a glimmer of secret knowledge and caustic humor. "There's something else I'd like to find," he said. To that frugal bait he added, "It's more important."

Shanter was silent. Watching his expressionless face, Wade thought "He knows something, but he'll never tell me. He's that kind." And then came comprehension. Deac Shanter would never step into any other man's personal affair. His was the code of the professional man of violence. Compassion for a friend had no place in it, but neither did betrayal of an enemy. The code stemmed from a deep and elemental conviction that every man must go forward on his own judgment, searching out the signs for himself and asking no help from the bystander.

He respected Shanter for that, but on a sudden decision he said, "Her name is Louise Venning."

He kept watching Shanter. A flick of sardonic amusement traveled up the hawk face. Shanter was letting it be known that he understood this game of baiting for an incautious slip.

"Last seen," Wade said, "she was traveling south over Raton Pass, in a rig with two men. The rig was a box buggy, bigger than most, with a top, and fitted with some kind of side curtains. They had to stop at a roadhouse. She was crying. The two men stayed out of the light. One was drinking. He had a rough temper. That's about all the roadhouse keeper saw. I think they put a scare in him so he made a point not to see too much."

"Sounds like an old story," Shanter observed.

"I'm not so sure. The girl was acting strange before she went missing. There's money and property behind her. She might not have gone off on her own accord. Peppy Martin told me she saw a girl like her one day, way west of Maya. In a buggy. Two men rode ahead. The man driving the buggy had a red face and white hair. He was thin and he wore some kind of Indian shirt. Max Luttrell, the Sheriff says."

"Was she your girl?"

Wade shook his head. "I've never laid eyes on Louise Venning. Only her picture. A lawyer gave me the job to find her. Name of Feenix, repping for her father. Her father put up the money. Two hundred for expenses, five thousand when I find her, dead or alive. They want to keep the thing hushed, no scandal."

"Understandable," commented Shanter. "But why you?"

"I've done jobs before for Feenix," Wade said. On that brief statement he let stand a record he was not proud of. "Feenix knows I've spent time in Mexico. They think that's where she's gone. But that's something else I'm not sure of."

He was silent, reflecting on the oddly virtuous nature of his quest in contrast to some of the things a desperate need for cash had made him do for Feenix. "The money doesn't mean so much now, but I should go through with the job." He was quiet again, and then he said, "I feel damn sorry for that girl."

Deac Shanter shrugged his big shoulders. "Meaning you'd kill the man if you found him? You'd have Hugh Stuart on your tail. He's tough."

Wade shot him a quick stare. "So you think I might find him here? And her?"

Shanter took up his glass, refilled it, drained it. He gazed past Wade. His eyes were contemplative, like those of a man making a reasoned play and giving it an approving after-study.

"Well, yes." He coughed gently on the whiskey. "Yes, Forrest, I wouldn't be surprised."

CHAPTER 3

THE MORNING GATHER having been rounded in, and dinner done with, the work of branding was begun. All morning since before daybreak the Gunsight men had been out, letting silence settle over the camp, until along toward noon a dark line broke into view in the distance. The line bunched and thickened with the charging of riders driving it forward, and cattle grazing near the camp lifted their heads in apprehension. Pinched shrill whoops pierced the constant battling of calves, bawling of cows, grumbling thunder of bulls. That was Concho Pace, sending out unrepressed Comanche yells.

Out of the furious boil of dust streamed the cattle, harried along by riders whose horses darted back and forth with the nimbleness of wildcats, turning rebel captives into line, keeping the line plunging on to the cutting ground.

In the cutting ground, the *parada*, they raised one tumultuous chorus, milling about, mother cows blaring for their calves while the bulls shoved and plowed and hooked sullenly at anything before them.

The cook sang out, "Come an' git it, you stinkin' jaspers!" and there was the wild ride to the chuck wagon. Twenty minutes later Arne Bassett clattered his tin plate and cup into the dishpan and said, "Let's get to work."

The Principe range being as it was—held by T Anchor, Gunsight and Bar V, with settled boundaries—each outfit conducted roundup on its own location. Still, it was open country, free range, bare of fence. Nothing hindered a cow from straying over the valley to try the grass on the other side. For that reason T Anchor had made it a rule to send a representative to attend all neighboring roundups, a rep rider whose job was to see that no calf belonging to his outfit got burned with the wrong brand.

Ordinarily, Wade guessed, the T Anchor representation wasn't much more than a formality. Bassett and Brouk, in bitter rivalry for Beth Tarey's favor, would lean backward in making sure that any calf possibly owned by T Anchor was correctly branded. T Anchor men were treated well at Gunsight and Bar V. It was said in the bunkhouse that they got first grab at the grub and big smiles all around.

Not so, in the case of Wade Forrest.

Arne Bassett, his brittle handsomeness roughened by three days' growth of beard, presented a hard stare when he had to speak to Wade. In his garb now there was nothing to distinguish Bassett from his men. Wearing faded and soiled Levis, flannel shirt, scuffed boots and a shapeless hat, he did his share, got as grimed in sweat and dust as the rest, and ran the works capably. And yet somehow he retained an air of dash and assured command. A stranger, coming up cold from far away, could pick him out at once as the boss.

Perse—his first name was Colin, so Wade learned—made it a rule to ignore Wade. But when he thought Wade wasn't looking, his milky blue eyes thinned to chips of concentrated malice. He kept his smashed nose greased to hold off dust, and a bandanna over it, tied road-agent fashion.

The rest of the Gunsight riders simply excluded Wade. He didn't exist for them. Concho Pace could strut his little-man swagger past him without a nod as if he had never seen him before, as if he remembered nothing of Wade's setting him up to drinks in Josefita's dive and again in Toland's Bar. The little Californian, in his tight black shirt and pants, huge silver buckle and studs, had the knack of staying always neat and dapper and smilingly insolent.

They would try today, Wade thought edgedly, to put something over on him. Not against T Anchor, but at him. He saw it coming, and regretted it. Some of these Gunsight riders, like Spud Temple or Bill Reese, he could have made friends with under better conditions. But of course they were loyal to Gunsight; to Bassett, the owner and big augur; and even to Perse, their range boss. They would back up their outfit and they were right, although most of them were only hired from spring to the winter lay-off.

And there was Concho Pace, whispering to them, making mock of the new T Anchor man, the rep rider who would be laid back and laughed at. And Perse, malevolent, gingerly readjusting the bandanna, hungry to collect tenfold for his broken nose. Arne Bassett, ready at any time to give the nod.

They were set to get him. Wade sat his horse and watched the cutting-out from the gathered day-herd, the branding and ear marking, the bloody rites performed with sharp knives and brawn and profanity. A branding ground, he mused, was a dirty, brutal place. It had to be so.

First, a rider cut a calf from the herd, chased it, roped it, dragged it up, its frightened mother bellowing and following.

"Gunsight!" barked the tally man, reading at a glance the brand on the mother.

The flanker caught his rope, slapped hard, jerked, and landed on the sprawled calf.

From the trenched fire came running the men with hot irons and knives, and when the busy huddle broke up, the calf had become a branded, ear-marked, future steer for the beef market, scrambling free to its bellowing mother. In half an hour, well licked, it would be nibbling contentedly, fright and hurt forgotten. The acrid white smoke of burned hair and hide hung in suspension with the dust, and grimed men spat and snorted it from their noses as they got ready for the next tussle.

"Gunsight!" came the call with the arrival of another spraddle-legged calf at the end of a rope tied short to the rider's saddlehorn. This was tie-fast country. They didn't use the dally.

"No," Wade said.

They all looked hard at him, then at the worried mother cow trying to dodge past a rider to follow her calf. Wade pointed his chin at the cow. "T Anchor."

"Hell, you can't see her brand from there!" a Gunsight man argued. The cow was head-on to Wade. The rider, Bill Reese, held it off at some distance, his horse blocking its brand from sight.

"I got her ear marks," Wade said. "Left overbit, right swallow-fork. Hey, Reese—bring her on!"

Bill Reese cracked his rope on the cow and drove her back into the herd, calling sourly, "T Anchor!"

The same thing was repeated four times in the course of the afternoon. They were laying for him and he wouldn't be caught and because of that their hostility heated to rage. Each time he challenged the call and hit it right, they branded and earmarked and knife-worked that calf savagely, taking it out on the animal. It was getting raw. His temper rose. His tongue got rough.

"Can't you fellows read brand?"

Concho Pace, relieving a man who got rope-burned, rode deeply into the herd and hauled a calf up close to the fire. "Gunsight!" he sang out.

The calf was a brindle, mahogany streaks on an unusually light brown background. A yellow brindle. Wade asked curtly, "Where's the cow?"

The flanker downed the calf. Pace retrieved his rope, coiled it and said with a glance toward Bassett, "She didn't come out o' the bunch. Hell, we all know that ol' brindle cow. She's a marker. Drops one like this every year."

Bassett nodded contemptuously and snapped, "Gunsight she is!"

Wade leaned forward slightly in his saddle. "I want to see the cow."

"I saw it. The critter's a marker, I tell you!" Pace's tone carried conviction. The faces of the waiting men mirrored the stormy indignation of liars accused of lying when for once they were telling the truth. Of course it was a Gunsight calf.

"Your word," Wade said, "just isn't enough for me."

He saw the wild brightness leap in Pace's eyes. He tightened his reins and rested his right hand on his thigh.

Concho Pace kneed his horse around and walked it toward him. "What do you mean?"

"I mean," Wade said, "this outfit's been trying to hooraw me all afternoon. I mean I don't take your word, nor the word of any Gunsight man here. I mean you'll play hell branding that calf for Gunsight unless you produce the cow. That clear to you?"

He let Pace ride up to within ten feet of him. The Gunsight hands had all risen to their feet, work suspended. Arne Bassett and Perse, too, were moving toward him. He looked carefully at Concho Pace and marked his intention, and on the first shift of Pace's hands he heeled his horse full at him.

For a moment they were two men balanced on rearing horses in collision. Wade swung far over and brought his drawn gun arching down smartly. The barrel crushed the peak of Pace's sombrero down to the silver-studded band. Pace uttered a thin, keening cry and his spooked horse bucked off and flung him.

Reining his horse down, Wade poked his gun at Bassett. "Snub it off. I've taken enough from your outfit. Snub it off, I say!"

Arne Bassett raised a frigid glance from Pace on the ground, to Wade, and they locked stares. He motioned to Perse to keep still. Perse edged forward and halted, watching Wade's gun.

Arne said to Wade, "You picked the wrong time for this play. That's a Gunsight calf." Then his anger pulled its peg. "You woman-chasing drunk, I'll see you run out or buried!"

CHAPTER 4

Riding with Deac Shanter on the hard seat of a T Anchor buckboard, Beth Tarey moved restlessly and Shanter commented, "I told you it's not a good road. Arne had some work done on it but the spring rains washed it out again. They never learn to slab-rock the ruts. Too much trouble."

He flicked the whip twice. As the lunge of the team threw Beth hard against the wooden seat-back, he added reflectively, "It's no pleasure jaunt, this road."

She sent him a side glance of wrathful dislike. "You drive like a maniac!"

She was bruised, in acute discomfort, and she suspected him of purposely slamming the off wheels on her side into the worst holes. He was entirely capable of it. He had said nothing against her request that he drive her over to Gunsight to see how the roundup was shaping up, but in his detached fashion he let her understand that it didn't meet with his approval.

She wished, not for the first time, that she could afford to fire Deac. The thought always conjured up a satisfying vision, a fantasy in which she said serenely, "T Anchor doesn't need you any more, Deac. Sorry. Tolfer has my order to give you three months' pay. Good-bye, Deac, and good luck."

He exasperated her so with his cool independence, his sardonic mockery of gravely listening to her wishes and then calmly disregarding them. His overpowering personality. Everything about him. In his presence she was inevitably and irately on the defensive. Often, alone, she muttered, "He's only a hired man, damn him. He just works for me."

But common sense warned her away from that. T Anchor needed Deac, and she knew it. So had her father known it, when he lay dying and conquered enemies came with their false sympathy. In his last letter to her, Simon had scrawled and underlined: *Don't ever break with Deac Shanter or you won't keep T Anchor long.*

As usual, he signed it, "Captain." That was the name, the title by which she always called him in fond respect. Rarely had there been a word of affection, for that was implied and unspoken.

He had brought her up much as he would have raised a son, aiming primary facts bluntly at her when needed, letting her learn intermediate lessons for herself. He had despised demonstrative emotion.

Damn Deac Shanter!

Captain, picking the best man as always, had sent to Tombstone asking the noted Deac Shanter to come and take on a delicate and dangerous job of cleaning out an expert rustling gang operating from west of Los Freyes— a daring bunch, protected by bought lawmen in their section. Deac had accomplished that in two weeks, saying merely on his return, "They won't bother you any more." And he claimed pay for six months, that much time having been agreed on for him to finish the task.

Captain paid the bill without complaint. He then offered Shanter a proposition to ramrod T Anchor. Shanter took three days to look the outfit over and accepted. He had never before worked for wages, he mentioned, but he'd taken a liking to tough old Captain and the outfit and guessed he'd make an exception.

The gall of the man!

"I'll hold this outfit together," he told Captain Simon Tarey, king of the Principe. "I'll bust anybody who ever tries to nibble at it or even looks like he's got a mind to. Anybody. But I want a free hand. If you ever cross my orders, I quit flat right then. If you want me, it's got to be that way."

And Captain, sick, grinned his tough grin and said, "You'll stick by that?"

"I'll stick to hell and yonder."

" 'Sta buen!" said Captain.

That last letter from Captain reached Beth in Paris. Her chronic discontent, for years nagging at her, came to a head. It was a time of scorn for everything American. She had given her share to that scorn, had described cruelly the crudities of ranch life, coloring it all with clever comedy that fetched chuckles from her listeners in pressed tailcoats and starched shirts. The letter, scratched in a wavering hand, a shaky caricature of Captain's generous scrawl, stabbed her. She took passage on the first ship home.

Captain was dead and buried when she reached T Anchor.

She had been abroad for years, and now she found the country new to her. She rediscovered it delightedly. It had rawness, yes, but the rawness of fresh vitality. Its people did not pour out words in fluent streams of facile subtleties. Speech here was carved down to bone-bare meanings. Men went openly armed as a matter of course, and many were more than half Indian in their plain thinking. An insult, however exquisitely phrased, could strike the flint in them and fire their tinder. This was rich wine to her, for her tastes depended largely upon a strong masculine compound. Without men around her she soon grew moody.

And here—also a dominant element in her appreciation —she stood as the acknowledged queen of a territory larger than many a European province. Being her father's child, she enjoyed thoroughly the privilege of brushing conventions aside. She built her house, Los Portales, just off Miles and a short hour's ride south of Maya; and there she startled the country with parties, magnificent parties unheard-of since the old days of the great grant-owning Spanish dons. On dull days she was known to order a stagecoach to stop and unload its fares for a few hours of hospitality. Her flashing charm, as much as her position, excused her impudence in upsetting the stage line's schedule. She did everything in the royal style, un-challenged—except when Deac Shanter regarded her sar-donically as if she were not a woman of the world, not Principe's queen, but just a flighty girl whose power had gone to her head. Sometimes Deac quite infuriated her. His look was enough, and he looked that way now.

"My driving," Deac observed coolly, lurching the buckboard through an old washout, "is an expression of my attitude. I'm not pleased with you, lady."

She held on to the seat, bitterly aware of her dust-powdered face and dress. Her fine white gloves were soiled. She had broken a finger nail. All this after starting out radiant.

"You're my ranch manager, Deac. Not *my* manager!"

"Not *your* ranch manager, either," he corrected. "It's

your ranch, but running it is my job. There's a distinction, lady."

"Captain hired you!"

"Your father, dear, offered me a deal, which I took. His death didn't affect it. We agreed to that." The faintest ghost of a smile touched the corners of Deac's mouth. "We got along. He was a damn good man, your father."

He said no more the rest of the way, until thick dust columned up over the next rise of hills. Then he pulled in the team and dropped a clean white handkerchief in her lap. "Here's the *parada*. Want to fix yourself up?"

That was another side to him. A kind side, casually understanding of women and their needs, that never failed to catch her off guard. He knew so damned much, the big devil.

Wordless, she stepped down from the buckboard and shook and brushed her dress, and when she had managed such repairs as she could he got out and handed her back up to the seat. It was very difficult then to see him as a gunfighter, as a killer with cruelly stretched nerves and no faith in anybody.

He took up the lines and hit the team, after lighting a cigar. His hands cupping the match were as steady as those of a man who had never known a night's unbroken sleep. In that instant Beth Tarey realized that Deac would stop at nothing to do his job, to hold T Anchor together. He had made that his cause and there wasn't the slightest scrap of uncertainty in him. She felt grateful.

They topped the rise and wheeled down to the *parada*, and the potential violence of the scene there drew a murmured word from Beth.

Arne Bassett and Perse and the Gunsight hands were closely eyeing Wade, who had his gun out. Concho Pace lay on the ground, hugging his head. Deac Shanter hauled in and queried mildly, "Having trouble here?"

Bassett trod stiffly to the buckboard.

"Beth, you know we'll go along with a T Anchor man any time. But this new duck you've chucked at us—God, he's outside all reason! He's claiming that's a T Anchor calf. We all know it's not. We know—"

"Get it straight," Wade broke in. "I claim the calf's a maverick till I see the cow." He looked at Deac Shanter.

Deac glanced at Pace. He could piece together all that

had occurred here. The pattern was predictable. Still, he stayed silent, impassive, smoking his cigar, waiting for Beth to say the wrong thing.

Beth said, "A calf? That's not worth fighting over. Take it if it's your's Arne."

Wade said, "If I'm repping for T Anchor, one calf's the same as a herd to me." He looked again at Deac, and said, "If that calf's branded without I see the cow, I ask for my time."

Now it was up to Deac, for Wade had put it right in his lap. Deac said, "Turn the calf loose."

The men holding it jumped clear. The yellow brindle calf ran back to the herd. It scampered past a Gunsight brindle cow which paid it no heed and crowded up against a yellow cow which accepted it. The yellow cow bore T Anchor ear-crops. The watching Gunsight men sucked their teeth and looked apologetically at Bassett. The calf was T Anchor.

Arne Bassett's handsome face washed red. He said, "All right, we allow it's T Anchor. But, Beth, this duck's whole attitude—he acts like he's God's brother!"

Wade said, "You're a liar," and dropped his right hand to his holstered gun.

Arne's color deepened. He stared tensely. Colin Perse shuffled forward, the devoted dog, willing and ready.

Deac said, "Now, now," and sat there on the buckboard seat, still quietly in command. He motioned to Perse, and Perse pulled back. "Hold it," he told Arne, and Arne froze.

"Let's not have any trouble," Deac said.

"How much d'you expect me to take?" Arne snarled. "You better pull him off, Shanter!"

Deac nodded. Wade reined his horse around ready to depart at once. Seeing the anger working in Wade's face, Deac said, "Bar V starts branding Friday, Forrest. I'd like you there."

It was a way of making plain that Wade's work had outright T Anchor approval.

"All right," Wade answered.

Beth Tarey went further. "I'm giving a birthday party, Saturday night," she said, smiling at Wade. "Come, won't you?"

He shuttled a glance to Deac, remembering the warning

that the hired hands were expected to keep their places as far as Los Portales was concerned. Deac was thoughtfully surveying the rocky upthrusts of Starvation Hills.

"Thanks," Wade said. "I'll try to be there."

"I'll expect you," Beth said. As if on afterthought she said to Bassett, "You, too, Arne." Then again to Wade, "Please tell Frank Brouk, will you?" Her eyes thanked him.

She clearly was under the impression that his stand in the matter of the brindle calf had been actuated by a jealous regard for her interests, rather than the ordinary stubborn squareness of a rep rider standing up for his outfit. He felt a stir of admiration for her grand conceit, as well as sympathy for her ignorance.

He caught Arne's rabid look and he said positively, "I'll be there."

CHAPTER 5

RIDING INTO MAYA the following Saturday afternoon, Wade debated whether to call at once on Catherine Larmor or first buy himself some presentable clothes for the Tarey party.

Pulling in at East Block, he remembered it was to be a birthday party. This called to mind a piece of Indian silver that had caught his eye in the tiny window of Wisely's jewelry and clock-repair shop. He racked his T Anchor horse and pushed open the shop door. The tinkle of the bell brought Wisely shuffling forward from the work cubicle at the rear.

"That Indian bracelet you had in the window a few days back—is it still for sale?"

"Everything I have is for sale." Wisely ran a look over this shabby puncher. "It's not cheap. Want to see it?"

"Want to sell it?"

Wisely smiled meagerly, got it from a drawer, and laid it on the counter. The bracelet was wrought of coin silver inset with blue turquoise, a handsome thing painstakingly hammered and bezeled and polished to a fine smooth luster by some Navajo master silversmith in his ill-lighted hogan.

"Very nice gift for a lady," Wisely murmured. "Rainbow God design. Believed to protect the wearer from all harm." He kept his eyes hooded under lowered lids.

Wade nodded absently, hoping Beth would like it. He paid, shoved it unwrapped into a pocket of his canvas brush-jacket, left the shop and turned the corner into East Street.

He glanced neutrally at the white-potted geraniums on the front gallery of the Larmor house, knocked on the door before opening it, was nearing the dining room when Katey bustled into the hall before him. Katey let a smile break through her dark mahogany dignity. "Mr. Forrest!" she exclaimed richly.

"Wade," he reminded her. "How've you been?"

"Just fine, Wade. Oh, Miss Catherine!" Katey paused, her smile deepening. "Here's Wade!" She stepped aside for him to pass into the dining room. Catherine came in from the kitchen and she, too, was smiling.

Curved and fair, strong arms bared to above the elbows and an apron over her house dress, she made him think again of a busy young housewife, still a bride. She was too constantly occupied running her boarding house to afford time to cultivate charm. Her hazel eyes had learned no tricks. They were as clean of guile as they must have been before she entered the age of feminine awareness. When the time came, her womanly vitality would easily find the power to incite and hold her man. She had not yet tapped that power, and would not until that time came.

She said, "Wade, how are you?"

Her use of his first name pleased him, although it had been forced on her by Katey. "I'm all right. You, Catherine?"

"Oh, yes. It's nice to—it's nice of you to call."

Katey said, marching to the kitchen, "Coffee."

They drank hot coffee at one end of the dining table. In just that there existed enough quiet intimacy to send Wade's thoughts wandering along unfamiliar paths. Except with Anna, in the neat little house in the little town to the north, it had never been his privilege to sit like this in the company of a quiet woman.

He had missed a lot in life. He had exchanged it, too

young to know the swindle, for another kind of life that had to be tough and hard to earn the needed cash. Johnny Gower, dying in the arroyo where his horse fell on him, had been too young to know what he was asking for his crippled sister. And he, Wade, had been too young to know what he was giving with his promise. "Why, Johnny, sure I'll take care of her, don't you wory. . . ."

A few words. Then the long years. The strain and struggle and hidden despair. A man's wild hunger for a whole woman.

Gentle Anna. He had been fond of her, had taken risks and won a bad reputation earning the considerable money it took to keep her in comfort. He thought of her alone in the little house, finally taking her way out through the sleeping medicine. That line of musing led back to hurt and he broke it off and said to Catherine more curtly than he intended, "I owe a bill here."

She must have been tracing his thoughts on his face, for she shook her head swiftly as if impatient with him. "Some time when you've drawn a few pays and you're on your feet. You need clothes and things. I can wait."

Sheriff Stuart had said that her boarders were her folks. Wade looked gravely at her. "I don't know how you keep this house paying on those lines."

She smiled at him. "I'm careful who I take in. They always square up some time."

He nodded slowly. "Take a poor kind of man not to. This morning Deac Shanter advanced me more than enough to set me up. Beth Tarey's giving a birthday party tonight. I couldn't go in the clothes I've got." He brought out the Indian bracelet and put it on the table. "D'you like this?"

She gazed down at it so long without speaking, he wondered if he had somehow committed an offense. Then she picked it up quickly and slipped it over her right wrist. "Very much," she said hushedly, and sat turning her wrist back and forth. "It's very lovely. I—wanted it so much when I saw it in Wisely's window, but I couldn't afford it."

At the kitchen door Katey uttered a coughing grunt. Flushing, Catherine raised her eyes from the bracelet to Wade's face. "Thank you, Wade. Shall I wear it to the party? It—it will go with my blue dress."

He was able to mask his face with grave pleasure. "Wish you would. I hoped you would." This still was not sufficient, and he asked, "Can I call for you around seven?"

"I'll be ready," she promised, in a voice shading to a whisper.

When Wade was gone, Katey came again to the kitchen door, filling it with her huge bulk. She said formidably. "You know he didn't mean that for you, Miss Catherine. That's no way for you to behave!" She stared scandalized at the fair girl sitting crimson-faced and slowly twisting the bracelet. Then her great dark eyes softened in pity.

Catherine came erect, squaring her shoulders.

"I wish you'd mind your own business, Katey Bloom! I know what I'm doing!"

At Harrison's Emporium on the main street, Wade sought the men's clothing section in the rear. To reach it he had to pass the hardware in front, and after that the tables of household and dress goods. It being Saturday, the store had other customers; but after scrimped nods the men paid him no heed, and the women bent absorbedly over the dress goods. As a T Anchor man he was entitled to some measure of deference, but as Wade Forrest he was personally branded as a woman-chasing drunk and a brawling hard-case.

Harrison himself trailed Wade to the rear—more out of curiosity than anything else, Wade guessed, for the man must have caught on to the significant silence of his regular customers. To the mention of a suit of clothes, Harrison shook his head in polite regret. A suit would have to be ordered from Denver . . . a month's delay, at least.

But he stood off and scanned Wade's large frame.

"Be glad to fix you up with something else, though. Nothing fancy, but quite presentable." He indicated his stock.

In the end Wade chose plain gray trousers, a white linen shirt and a coat that somebody his size had ordered and never called for. His hat and boots would have to do. Harrison, because he liked ready-money men who didn't haggle over price, threw in a black necktie and stated sincerely, "There, sir, you're fixed up for any occasion short of the governor's ball. Some men don't need fancy trappings." He seemed to take a sly relish in striking off at the back-turned disapproval of his less interesting customers, for he added, "Any lady should be proud to be seen with you, sir. Please give my best respects to Miss Tarey."

Wade settled his bill and from there went to Toland's Hotel with his wrapped purchases. To the young clerk he said, "How much for a room to change clothes in, and a bath?"

The clerk raised his brows and quickly lowered them. "One dollar. Room seven. The bath's downstairs, back."

Wade paid the dollar and took the key. Climbing the stairs, he looked back, something in the clerk's manner disturbing him. A couple of men in lobby chairs were peering up after him. So was the clerk, leaning over his desk, a lively inquisitiveness brightening his bored eyes. He entered room seven thoughtfully, dropped his bundles on the bed, and rolled a cigarette to think things over. But it was now getting late, so after a few drags he shrugged and went in search of the bath.

By seven o'clock, when he drew the red-wheeled buggy from Wright's Livery up before the Larmor house, the sun had passed below the peaks of Los Freyes. The unclouded sky was a darkening blue turning to purple-gray in the east. It was not yet quite light-up time in Maya but the gallery lantern already had been lighted above the steps and under the roof.

Wade's boots struck the first step. Katey threw the door wide and called, "Miss Catherine, here's Wade!"

Her smile at Wade was less than the smile he knew. At once he was on guard and he halted on the top step. The hall filled behind Katey, who moved aside. Catherine came out a little hurriedly. She was followed more slowly by a dozen men, her boarders. They emerged onto the gallery, eyeing Wade soberly.

It reached him then—the shocking knowledge. Had he been a woman he would have recognized it from the first. It had peered at him from the eyes of Wisely, of Harrison and the hotel clerk and all the others. The eyes all had asked in various humors, "You woman-chaser, who are you after now?"

He removed his hat to Catherine, while the sudden fill of knowledge pressed on, seeking an outlet concerning her. She was lovely in her blue dress, the bodice close-fitting and the skirt full and wide, the Navajo bracelet shining on her wrist, her fair hair piled high.

He knew what trouble she had gone to, from remembrance of Anna's interminable sessions in her room. He handed Catherine carefully down the gallery steps. Her arm felt cold to his hand. An elderly man among the boarders said kindly, "You have a good time, Catherine, a *good* time," and his eyes were steady on her.

This was a rare occasion, so rare in her day-after-day work to keep them fed and comfortable that they felt compelled to troop out and see her off. Wade was glad he had hired Wright's best rig. He was glad when Catherine, halting on his arm, said breathlessly, "Oh! And the gray team!"

She turned her fair head. "Katey! The gray team!" She was very like a child overwhelmed, and Katey called down to her from the gallery, "Yes, Miss Catherine, I see." And, discarding her Boston grammar, Katey said almost belligerently, "The best ain't none too good!"

Handing Catherine up into the buggy, Wade said directly to Katey, "I'd have got gold horses if I could." He walked around the fine gray horses, touching and rubbing them, and climbed up beside Catherine. "All right?"

"Yes, thank you."

He shook the lines. The well-trained team pulled away into the main street and swung left, between good East Block and bad West Block, past the fringe of shacks and out of town onto Miles Trail.

They rode the way scarcely speaking, meeting the night and its rustle of wind blowing up off the desert below Black Walls. It was dark by the time they reached Los Portales. The house stood about a hundred yards back off the stage road. It was built of plastered adobe. Several doors let out onto a wide flagstone portico lighted by hanging brass lanterns and furnished with painted Mexican tables and chairs. Light poured from every window on all sides of the house so that from the road it resembled a huge lamp. It was by far the grandest residence between Arco and Ute City. More than twenty rooms, it was said, not counting the three guest houses.

The fence fronting the yard had already filled up with rigs and horses. He made space for the buggy, carried the lines down and tied up, and handed Catherine to the ground. Her fingers lay unrelaxed in his palm. She was taut. He gave her his arm and escorted her to the main door open on the portico.

Here was the main room, larger than Toland's dance hall, splendidly furnished, full of people and talk and noise, a Mexican *típica* orchestra strumming softly. This was wealth, careless extravagance. This was Beth Tarey's house.

"Well, hell-*o!*" It was like singing. Deep in the throat. Warm, caressing.

She wore a gown of some silvery green stuff, like velvet and like silk. It was not the green of her jade eyes. Rather, it enriched her eyes by its moderate hue, heightened the contrasting glow of her chestnut hair, and brought out the creamy fineness of her skin.

Wade said to Beth, "Happy birthday."

Among the dozen young men trailing her, one chuckled in the loose confidence of drink, "Happy birthday every month for Beth!" And Wade was glad that he hadn't fished out his gift and made a fool of himself. He was grateful to Catherine, wearing it. He remembered her tautness at the door, and his knowledge spread out.

To Catherine, Beth stretched forth both hands and said warmly, "So glad you came, dear." She held Catherine's hands, smiling, giving them an affectionate little shake. "I want so much to know you better. Everybody speaks so nicely of you."

She cocked her head and surveyed Catherine. "You're quite, quite lovely, dear. This bracelet," she said, "was made for you. I can't imagine how that horrid little Wisely gets hold of such nice things."

So it was known, Wade thought uncomfortably. It was known that he had bought the bracelet. Maya was a gossip town where they added two and two and summed five. God, how fast a word could travel. Gossips and liars were twins.

He heard Beth saying gently to Catherine, "I'm sure you know everybody here, dear. Everybody knows *you.* May I?" She touched Wade. "The first dance. If you don't mind?"

The young men fell away, looking Wade up and down in his cheap clothes. His cheap clothes suited him. Plain black and gray and white, they framed correctly his remote look of casual dignity.

"Why, of course," said Catherine, smiling back, "dear."

By some motion that Wade barely caught, Beth put the *típica* orchestra to strumming over the noise. The noise subsided and the floor cleared. He led Beth out and danced with her.

It was the *varsoviana*. The old dance of Mexico and the Spanish Southwest. When he was very young and without cares he had danced it with pretty and pliant Mexican girls, taking the opportunity of the whirl-around to hold them strongly and make love to them. So long ago. He and Johnny Gower, crossing over the border, half dead from the racing exhaustion of combing wild mavericks out of the brush, coming alive again on cantering into San Juan or the settlements of Rio Humbardo.

Put your little foot—put your little foot—
Right there!

He danced it out with Beth all the way to the final big whirl, his right arm holding her while her toes skimmed inches above the floor. He saw Sheriff Stuart, too old for such acrobatics, walk to Catherine and speak to her. Surrounded now by men young and old, she shook her head.

The next dance, a slow Spanish waltz, began immediately.

"Shall we go on?" Beth murmured.

"Sure," he said.

He lost sight of Catherine in the crowd. The crowd pressed with new arrivals. Beth said to him, frank regret tinging her voice, "I suppose I should say hello to them." She was flushed and a little breathless, and her eyes sparkled.

He said, "Shanter's doing that for you." He kept his arm around her waist.

She swung readily to him, her eyes clinging to him, as disregardful as he of the attention they were creating. Arne Bassett was prowling gloomily about the packed room, trying without success to catch Beth's eye. Concho Pace, his tall black sombrero tipped forward because of his bandaged head, looked in at an open window on the portico. He leaned on the sill as if he had been stationed there.

Arriving late, Frank Brouk was met at the door by Deac Shanter. While they shook hands, Wade saw Brouk send out a ranging glance that quickly found Beth. Switching to him, it hardened. Frank would not waste time prowling around. He would come dead-on and bull it through. That was his style and he had the looks for it—a big brown-faced man, solidly impressive. Whether or not he had the equipment, he had at least the front.

Deac Shanter spoke with him, delaying him there at the door, drawing him aside as a special guest. In a moment Frank Brouk bent his head, listening to Deac.

CHAPTER 6

"It won't do you any good," Deac Shanter told Frank Brouk. "You don't stand a chance. Nor Bassett, either. Look at 'em. That's the fourth dance in a row. Look at Beth!"

Deac nipped a fresh cigar and put a match to it, his deep-set eyes wintry and wryly philosophical. "Frank, she's gone for him. You and Arne are through. We're done played."

Frank cursed. Then, remembering he was a big man, he shrugged like Deac and made his eyes blank. "We? How d'you mean, we?"

Deac Shanter passed him a cigar. "Why, hell, Frank, I mean you and Arne—and me. Yeah, me. Don't act dumb with me, man, I know you better than that."

Complimented, Frank nodded profoundly. He said, "Sure, I see what you mean." But he didn't see it.

Deac Shanter gave him a knowing nod. Privately, Deac had checked off Frank as a would-be big man who never would be big unless through sheer dumb luck. There was a flaw in him. For a while he had come very close to winning Beth, so close that everybody expected an announcement and Arne Bassett left with a beef herd for Wyoming delivery, to get away from the talk. But somehow Frank bobbled his great chance to be king of the Principe. He was by turns too brashly assured and too cautious, the pendulum of his courage swinging from one to the other. He had let Beth see that flaw, and it was fatal.

"Beth's mind is made up," Deac told him. "He's the one, take it from me. And he's no fool. He'll be boss. He wouldn't have it less, if I size him right. Nor would she. But he'll have to show he's got the weight, of course. How? It's a plain cinch. He'll move against Arne and run him out, first thing, soon as he gets Beth and T Anchor behind him. He and Arne are on horn-tossin' terms."

"That," Frank observed, "will suit me fine."

"It would," Deac agreed, "if he stopped at that. You figure he will? Would you? No, Frank. You'll be next, after Arne. To ride that high saddle he'll have to push and grab 'til all the grass in sight is T Anchor. It's the game he's got to play—or he'd soon be known as Mr. Tarey. You know that."

His optimism shattered, Frank growled, "I get it. Sure. Driftin' puncher marries cattle queen. All of a sudden he's king and he's got to show it. Sure." He chewed fiercely on his cigar. "Deac, that's something you haven't done. Moved in on High Folds, I mean. It'll build him a big record, bigger than yours. So—where'll it put you?"

Reading the turn, Deac replied with a shrug, "When she marries him I'll be all through here. That time's bound to come, whoever she marries. There's no room for two ram-rods in any outfit."

Frank started to speak, hesitated, and brought out the carefully hedged words Deac expected. "There'll always be room for you at Bar V. Any time, Deac."

"Thanks." Deac gazed out over the room. "But I'm used to a big outfit. You've only got a ten-man crew, plus maybe ten of your neighbors on the Starvations that would back you in a fight—if it was to their advantage."

"More. Fifteen, maybe twenty."

"Maybe. It's not enough." Deac shook his head. "No, I couldn't sit there waiting to be run off. I'd have to be pushing out, making your outfit big enough to stand him off. Pushing him back, come to that, and taking T Anchor grass. I play to win. The stakes here are the Principe. I'd play for that."

That planted it. He let it bloom, until inevitably Frank Brouk glanced around and muttered, "How?"

Deac drew his dark brows together impatiently. "Why, I'd take Gunsight first thing. Range and buildings. Not the cows. Taking the cows would pull Stuart in. The range, that's diff'rent. As I know, your Bar V used a lot of that Gunsight range before the boundary was settled. Right?"

"Sure, but Simon Tarey set the boundary and we all agreed—"

"The hell with that. Simon wasn't God, and he's dead now. Far as the law's concerned, your Bar V can claim prior rights to Gunsight range. Not much Stuart could do, once the thing's done, so long as there's no killing. All right, suppose Bar V grabs all High Folds. Right away you've got the Starvations cowmen backing you. They'll back the winner every time, as long as it's to their advantage, and I'd see to that. I'd give 'em the right to graze down into High Folds. I'd give 'em the right to water, which they sure do need. They'd fight to keep it so. They'd take my orders. About fifty of 'em, all told, besides your own crew. Why, with a fighting bunch that size I'd make Bar V the big outfit of the Principe!"

Deac Shanter was laying it out straight, outlining what *he* would do in Frank's case. His lean code prohibited lies, and within that limit he was not misleading Frank. It did not disturb his tough conscience to realize that Frank would be much more likely to meet disaster on that truthfully defined course than on a less daring one.

For Frank, despite his impressive appearance, was lightweight and Deac knew it. And, knowing it, Deac was untroubledly ready to watch Frank go to smash. Every man was entitled to the right to go forward on his own judgment. If the man's judgment was faulty, that was his own affair. His spill had to come some day. This was a country of hard living. It was no place for fools and four-flushers.

Deac watched Frank think it over. Frank was already accepting it as his own grand vision. It was betrayed by the gleaming of his large brown eyes, the boldening of his mouth and square jaw. Frank was dreaming dreams of greatness.

Deac glanced away and saw Arne Bassett watching them.

These two, Deac thought with a tinge of contempt, had

been stalking Beth like hounds in heat ever since she became mistress of T Anchor. Neither was truly in love
with her. Her personality had a force that did not grain
with their ideas of a submissive wife. Their courtship
stemmed from the hope of security, wealth, power. A
cheap ambition, because there could be no security for
their kind. Damn them to hell.

Frank said at last, "Yes, Deac, there'll always be room
for you at Bar V." His promise came lamely at the drag-
end of his thoughts. His mind was grappling with the
greater vision. He could not give credit. He could not
come out with a straightforward proposition fairly recognizing worth and offering profit. "See you later, Deac."

And even in this minor act he was too eager. He shouldered out through the front door to the portico, his expression that of an untrained poker player drawing a
straight flush. The cards had been stacked for him, but in
his self-flattering glow of cleverness he could not acknowledge the part played by the dealer.

Tinhorn!

Out of the corner of an eye Deac saw Arne Bassett turn
his face to Concho Pace at the window and rub both
brows. An old signal: Watch that man. Concho Pace
withdrew his elbows from the sill, swung around lan-
guidly to face the portico, and then moved off. Gone,
Deac knew, to follow Frank Brouk and learn what he was
up to. Pace would find out all about it.

Concho walked the length of the lighted portico and
around the south corner, small and unobtrusive in his
close-fitting black garb, and from there he drifted into
the *piñon* and juniper. At no time did he lose sight of
Frank Brouk, who searched quickly among the punchers
on the portico and jerked his head mysteriously to his
foreman.

The Bar V foreman, Happy Jack Liscow, so named
because of his unbreakably gloomy face, weaseled away
from a group of drinking punchers and trailed Frank to
the Bar V buckboard at the front fence. Happy Jack was
long and thin and he suffered a stomach ailment. He
wore a drooping black mustache that paralleled the down-
curve of his mouth. Although he never smiled, his thin
lips could display every emotion from sullen glumness to

sour satisfaction. His eyes were bloodshot, especially the left eye, which had a crimson cloud on it.

They climbed into the Bar V buckboard. Frank said in a hoarse whisper, "Jack, get the boys. We take back our Gunsight range tonight."

Jack Liscow's red left eye glared. "Take Gunsight? You drunk?"

"No. It just came to me." Frank nudged him. "Bassett's here and so's his crew. Bar V has prior right to that range, so we take it back. Stuart can't do a damn thing, long as there's no killing. And there won't be. What can Bassett do with only a few men? Hell, he's in trespass. Let's move in!"

It took Happy Jack a few moments to grasp it. He said then in his habitual whine, "What would Shanter do? Ol' Simon drew the boundary."

"Shanter's with me," Frank assured him. "I fixed that. When we show what we can do, he'll side us. He's through here. And he's worth twenty T Anchor hands, once we get him with us."

Happy Jack blinked his red eye. "You let Deac in, he'll own Bar V. He's bad medicine."

Frank took a shuddering breath. "We'll take care of him. Let him help us first, then take care of him. That's the ticket."

"I don't like it, Frank."

"Damn it," Frank exploded, "you got to like it! Get the boys. I know what I'm doing. Stick with me, you'll rod the big spread of the Principe. Shanter's in, I tell you. He'll side us as soon's we take Gunsight."

Twisting his lips into many phases of doubt, Happy Jack eventually nodded. "We could take Gunsight, yeah. They're all here. If we could be sure o' Shanter—"

"You can be sure! He's with us, I tell you!"

Deac spotted Concho as soon as he reappeared at the portico window. Concho touched his nose—another old signal—and Arne made his way out of the house, nodding to Deac in passing. Deac brushed along the wall and all who saw him coming made way for him. He extended courtesy to all. A grave nod. A few words. Nobody ever attempted to buttonhole him when his manner forbade it. He could freeze off the most drunken man with a glance.

Wade had just said to Beth, "Maybe you *should* give

'em a hello, eh?" And she had murmured regretfully, "Maybe I should."

They stopped at a table where a Mexican of exquisite politeness served them drinks. Wine for Beth. Whiskey for Wade. She said, smiling up at him over her glass, "Take care of yourself," not knowing that in this country those words couched a clear warning.

When Beth left Wade, Deac came up and said briefly, "I hate to spoil the party, Forrest, but there's a job for you."

"You're the boss," Wade said, putting his drink down. Shanter had been pretty good to him, advancing him more pay than any puncher could rightly expect. "I'm ready any time."

Deac liked that. He inclined his head in acknowledgment. "We've got what was a line camp, used to be a ranch, down by Black Walls. About two miles east of the road. A trail cuts off to it. We don't use the place now, 'count of the grass-blight down there, but you can't miss it. Some jigger is squatting there, I hear. A squaw man. See about it, will you? His name is Luttrell."

"Max Luttrell?"

"Yeah," Deac drawled, "that's him. You want any help?"

"No."

"Well, I didn't figure you would. By the way, I hear he's got a buggy there, a big one with a top and canvas side-curtains. That's not usual for a nester."

"It's not," Wade said. He looked the room over.

"Miss Catherine Larmor," Deac informed him, "has been taken home by Sheriff Stuart. Which leaves you free. You take my horse. I'll see your rig back to Wright's."

Deac Shanter watched Wade leave. He lit a fresh cigar, but when Beth came up after saying her hasty greetings to her guests Deac dropped the cigar and crushed his heel on it.

"Where's everybody?" Beth demanded. "Arne's gone, and Frank. And now Wade. Damn it, Deac, what are you up to?"

He took her hand. "May I have this dance with you, lady?"

He whirled off onto the floor with her, as graceful as a

dancing master. The heavy guns under his coat did not bob and intrude their dark presence into the feline smoothness of his steps. He smiled down at her and for once his eyes came unmasked. Utterly ruthless eyes, yet kind now. He was gentle and courtly, and he said to her, "I'm never gone, lady. I'm here to stick to hell and yonder."

CHAPTER 7

ALTHOUGH silent travel was ruled out by the creak of leather and the shuffling trot of the horses on hard ground, the Bar V hands rode mute-tongued through the night, the grim earnestness of their mission suppressing any desire for speech.

When starting out they had ridden single file and been less taciturn. Now, on Gunsight range, they bunched up like wary Indians entering unfamiliar territory. The moon, three-quarters full and high, allowed them to view the vast sweep of the valley below High Folds clear to Los Freyes rearing blackly in the west.

It had taken longer to gather in all hands than Frank had figured. And only four young men from Starvation Hills had responded to his summons to join his crew. The four swore more were coming, but they didn't show up. While waiting for them at Bar V, Frank took on several drinks and finally called out, "Hell, there's enough of us. Let's go!"

Riding in the front with Happy Jack, Frank asked his foreman, "Got anything to drink with you?" Happy Jack shot him a somber look and shook his head. Frank muttered, "It don't matter."

His sharp edge of optimism had worn off. The pendulum was swinging back. He was conscious of uneasiness in the men. It angered and pricked him with doubts. In the bright lights and music and happy noise of Los Portales, talking with Deac, this thing had glowed, splendidly feasible. Deac had made him feel that he was a big man, well able to pull it off. He would take what he wanted. He would be master of High Folds at one bold stroke. Defy the power of T Anchor. Break T Anchor. Have Beth come begging to him.

In the cold moonlight the aspect altered. Happy Jack's morose pessimism had communicated itself to the men. The weight of this thing pressed wholly on him, Frank. Possible bobbles and dire consequences kept occurring to him. He began seeing this venture as a desperate gamble. Pride was all that held him from calling it off. He had proposed it as his own idea, had pushed and bulled the men into participating. He was committed to it.

There was a thin chance that Beth's party had broken up earlier than usual, and that Arne Bassett and his crew were now at Gunsight. In that case the invasion was off. No veneer of legality could justify an armed attack. Frank Brouk couldn't admit it to himself, but he hoped there would be lights at Gunsight. He stared hard ahead, leading his reluctant troop over the last bench.

No lights shone from Gunsight. The buildings occupied a treeless draw, at the head of which some seep springs ran from a gravel ridge to form a pool. There was the bunkhouse, kitchen at one end. Stables and corrals below. Facing the main house across the bare yard stood Bassett's office, a shack. The wagon shed was off to the north side. A plain working outfit, this.

The Bar V invaders pulled in to eye it thoroughly in the moonlight, frowns betraying their discontent. Frank heaved a breath and said, "Happy, ride on down and hail the house. If they come out, run for it."

"I won't wait to shake hands, that's for sure."

Happy Jack touched his horse forward and grew small down the slope. He drew within fifty yards of the bunkhouse, reined half around, and they heard him sing out. The lonely sound of his voice raised a weak echo from the gravel ridge and that was all; but he sat listening, swinging his head, scouting the Gunsight buildings that roughly squared the empty yard. While silence congealed he bent over and peered toward the horse corrals, trying to make out if any of the horses there had been ridden recently.

Sudden reaction sank Frank's load of worry and he released a breath, covering it with a laugh. Happy Jack's shy prudence aroused in him a deep contempt. Hell,

Happy didn't have the sand to ramrod a tough, up-and-coming outfit like Bar V.

"Nobody home," Frank announced, so loudly that he startled the men. He threw his right arm up and forward. "Let's go."

He led them down at a gallop. They caught the new mood of confidence. A youthful puncher from the Starvations raised a whoop.

Happy Jack whirled around, shaking his head helplessly. His horse danced. He struck it on the head with the butt of his quirt.

"My God, Frank, are you crazy?"

Frank shouted at him, "You dismal dandelion! Any fool can see there's nobody home! We're moving in!"

There was nothing else for Happy to do but ride along. The young Starvations puncher let out another whoop. Their hoofs pounded on the hard-beaten surface of the yard. There they reined in short. Through the dust-roiled moonlight they stared about them and for that moment they were hard-case riders on a raid, guns ready and eyes on fire.

But it was a mood that had to run a brief course. They were working punchers first, scrappers second. In this land where rough living made for rough tempers, they were no rougher than average. In the absence of anything definite to feed on, their ferocious mood could not be sustained. It sagged, and a hush came over them, and they waited for Frank to head the next move.

The time then was ripe. From his Gunsight office Arne Bassett called blandly, "C'mon in, Frank."

Somebody in the wagon shed chuckled grimly and let the bolt of a rifle be heard locking into the breech. That lean snick of sound repeated in the shed and along the open windows of the bunkhouse. The Bar V invaders shrank together, trapped in the bare, moonlit yard.

Happy Jack sighed a lugubrious oath. Expecting the worst, he spun his horse and made a run for it. A Winchester repeater at the end of the bunkhouse slashed fire twice. The gravel ridge sent back two flat echoes, but did not return the softer noise of Happy Jack's floundering fall.

"Up with the hands! Make it quick!" That was Perse's harsh whine.

And then a crooning drawl from little Concho Pace. "Show the paws, you hairpins, an' let 'em be clean!"

Arne Bassett came to the door of the Gunsight office. He didn't trouble to carry his gun in his hand. He still wore the good clothes he had donned for Beth's party. With his brisk manner they lent him an odd appearance of formality.

He tipped a hand to Brouk. "Light down and come in, Frank. We've been waiting for you." The dry and mocking manner didn't quite fit him. He was too brittle by nature.

Frank dismounted woodenly, grounded the reins and stood looking at Arne.

"Step inside, neighbor." Arne lifted Frank's gun from him. "Reese! Temple! Over here. Perse, you look after these."

Reese and Temple came from the bunkhouse. They trotted across the yard and entered the office behind Frank. Arne followed them in, and a light came on and he closed the office.

Perse bulked from the wagon shed with Pace. Others stepped from the bunkhouse. Perse said, "Get their guns, Concho." A minute or two later Concho Pace said, "What a collection. Would you b'lieve it, some o' these pilgrims still tote those ol' cap-an'-ball guns. Ain't it a shame?"

By then the closed Gunsight office was noisy. It resounded with thuds, cries. Some articles of furniture crashed. The cries sank to moans.

Bassett said something commandingly. There came another protesting groan, more thuds. Then silence.

After a short time Arne opened the office door. Reese and Temple, both big men, helped Frank Brouk out into the yard. Frank sagged between them, moaning softly. His clothes were torn and rumpled, and his face had been beaten to a bloody pulp. When they released him he fell to his knees.

Arne said to the disarmed men, "Pick him up and get out of here. Don't go back to Bar V. Frank's turned that range over to me, with all improvements and livestock thereon, for certain considerations, signed and witnessed. You're driftin'. So's he. He might make another start somewhere, but not in the Principe. He's all through here and he knows it."

The Gunsight men watched them boost Frank up onto his horse, and, with a man on each side supporting him, ride wordlessly out of the yard. They took Happy Jack along as well, slung over his saddle.

Looking slowly from one face to another of his men, Arne said, "High Folds is all Gunsight range now. The Starvations will back us, soon as it's known Frank's quit." He was attempting an expressionless manner, but a kind of wildness rang through his tone. "For the looks of it I'll give Stuart a story. He won't believe it, but there's nothing he can do."

"How's Shanter goin' to take it?" Perse asked.

Frowning off into the darkness, Arne answered, "We'll drop by Los Portales and find out. Guess the party's still on. I can't quite figure Shanter's game, giving Frank the go-ahead, but I think this is about what he expected. No, somehow I don't look for trouble there. What bothers me is that damned Forrest. He's getting way up out of his class."

Perse snuffled his greased nose and growled, "Leave him to me. I got a tall score to settle with him."

"And me," put in Concho Pace, smilingly baring the knot on his head. "*Por favor*, count me in on that, eh? How far can we go?"

"All the way," Arne murmured. "I don't give a damn how you do it, just so you don't leave sign for Stuart."

CHAPTER 8

Riding Deac Shanter's good bay horse, Wade Forrest crossed the Calaveras shallow ford below the adobe ruins of old Fort Miles and thereby quit the stage road for a southeast-bent trail. From there on the country was new to him, though familiar in its broad pattern. The trail angled off toward the low benches south of High Folds, between Bar V range and Black Walls. Cow tracks and dimmed wagon ruts showed that it was not being traveled much.

Circle 7, one of the ranches acquired by T Anchor in

Simon Tarey's time, was not being used this year because of the grass blight there. That, however, gave no permit to squatters to make free with the buildings on it. If Max Luttrell was camping at Circle 7 with his Indian bunch, T Anchor had every right to throw him off.

It was like Deac Shanter, Wade mused, to take that oblique reason to send him down to Circle 7—knowing very well that if Luttrell was hiding the big buggy there that had borne the missing Louise Venning down from the north, that made it his, Wade's, personal affair.

On the other hand, he reflected narrowly, it was not like Deac to bulge in on what didn't concern him. A motive generally lurked somewhere behind the actions of such a man. Deac also had sent him to rep for T Anchor at the Gunsight roundup, where it was a steel cinch he'd run head-on into trouble from Arne Bassett and his hostile crew. Max Luttrell had gone Indian. Bad Indian, from all accounts. He'd give trouble.

Wade recalled how Sheriff Stuart had warned him against riding for T Anchor. Stuart knew a thing or two that he didn't care to spill. That tired, shabby, coldly efficient old lawman was ready to let mischief go by, unmentioned, in preference to the savage flare-up of a range war. He knew the people of this violent land, knew much of their secrets and desperate ambitions, and in his aged wisdom the foremost pillar of his creed was peace. He had seen too much bloodshed.

Thinking of Stuart turned Wade's mind, shamed, to Catherine. It was a cruel thing he had done, deserting her like that at Beth Tarey's party, leaving her alone and embarrassed in her pretty dress and trying with pitiful gallantry to hide crucified pride behind a too bright smile while he danced and paid open court to Beth. Until at last Stuart rescued her and took her home.

His neglect of her had been deliberate, wholly in her interest. She was neither Peppy Martin, a dance hall girl careless of her reputation, nor Beth Tarey, an aristocrat who could afford to shrug off propriety. Running a boarding house for men, Catherine needed to be more circumspect in her behavior than most young women.

He had suddenly realized, at the door of Los Portales, her purpose in appearing publicly with him. She was simply staking her own reputation in an effort to win him some measure of Maya regard and respectability. It was a grand and generous gift that he could not accept from her. He could not let her take that risk, and so he had deliberately cut himself away from her.

But the guilt of it lay hard on him, one more unhappy ghost to live with the rest of his life. He felt bitter.

The trail, after another one crossed it east and west, grew fresher, scored by more recent travel. Black Walls loomed up.

He pulled in, wondering if by some chance he had missed Circle 7. But the trail ran on. He followed it forward and presently made out the straight edge of a roof among the weird contortions of Black Walls. The massive waves of volcanic black basalt, cooled and hardened in grotesque shapes writhing as high as fifty feet and extruding from the valley floor for twenty miles, resembled a giant graveyard in the moonlight. According to Navajo legend the lava was in fact the blood of a giant slain by the war gods of the Zuñis.

He turned the bay off the trail, walked it about a quarter-mile westward and drifted in among the lava rocks. He grounded the reins, knowing that any horse Shanter owned would stand ready without tying. He had a cowpuncher's dislike of footwork, but a greater objection to riding into a bullet, so he took bearings and started through the black maze to strike Circle 7 from, he hoped, an inconspicuous entrance.

In an hour he gained respect for the known ability of Black Walls to swallow up and lose a man. Down here at the bottom all sense of direction was lost. A man could go round in circles. Four times he had to back up, consult the moon-shadows high above, and make a radical change of course. And always, the oppressive dead silence. No night swallows. No faint rustle of brush. Nothing but the black, dumb, insane shapes tearing eternally upward at nothing.

A light flickered. In his relief he swore softly and hurried on. He grazed his knee against a chunk of basalt. He wished he had brought the carbine from his saddle. He had only his gun, a single-action .44. It wouldn't do to break up this nest.

The flickering light came from a fire in the Circle 7 yard. It burned before the open flaps of an old army tent.

The ropes of the tent sagged unevenly. The tent sat askew. One of its seams had split. Men sat hunched around the fire. He counted eight.

He took his inspection off them and raked it over the whole layout. The yard was bounded by the rocks. A gap in the rocks formed the entrance. There was a tumble-down bunkhouse, apparently not in use, for it was dark. A small shed, likely the spring-house. Rock-walled corrals held a few horses. The main house had two floors, un-common in this country. It had once been painted white with *yeso*. Flakes still clung to show that. There were lights in the downstairs windows and a single one above. But for the Indian camp in the yard, it could have been the quiet home ranch of any working outfit.

He was thirty feet above ground and he pondered the problem of getting down. He backed up and went search-ing and found a crevice that descended and offered him a short jump. He dropped down lightly and walked, look-ing back carefully to establish in his mind the shapes of the two rocks through which he had emerged. The one on the left was a tall slab without distinguishing features. The one on the right extended a beak and cleft below that. It reminded him of Deac Shanter and so he named it.

Keeping as far as possible from the fire and the house, he prowled around the yard to the corrals. Moonlight edged the east side of the yard, but the west side lay in the shadow of the high rocks. He buttoned his coat over his shirt and turned the collar up. The slack figures at the fire didn't move.

Near the corrals a rough shelter had been constructed in a crevice of the black rocks, a lazy man's slipshod job of unpeeled logs wedged across the crevice to form a roof, brush and dirt piled on top. He turned and explored it. Brush had been thrown up at the entrance, but some had settled and fallen away, so he was able to peer over it. A big buggy stood in there. It had a canvas top and side curtains.

He thought of Peppy Martin and what her information to him had cost her. He hoped Peppy had found a soft champagne-and-velvet spot somewhere.

A door of the house banged noisily and a voice called out something ending in the slurred phrase, ". . . *a-ye-na!*"

The figures around the fire rose, their faces intent upon

a man shambling toward them from the house. The man carried a stone jug and he was white. Even in the poor light he bore the look of a gambler broken all the way down. His one-time splendor of broadcloth and linen was tattered and soiled to scarecrow poverty. He did not fit the description of Max Luttrell.

"*Baiya. . . !*" came a hoarse shout.

These were Navajo men, then, these beggarly tramps. Wade shook his head in angry pity. By the same scales that measured the derelict gambler as a white man, they were Navajos. On all other counts they were whiskey-sodden outcasts. They grinned bare-toothed at the jug like starved wolves at the smell of blood. Firm and haughty Navajo features had degenerated to ruined mouths gaping from corrupt faces.

Each had a rifle. This relic badge of manly menace had to be dug forth from the filthy blankets and flourished to the man carrying the jug. He nodded. He set the jug down on the ground as he reached the fire, and tried with drunken playfulness to sit himself on it. They made wheedling sounds to him. The jug rolled out from under him, letting him sprawl. He laughed, staggered to his feet and kicked the jug toward them. Then he waved his arms and rocked back to the house. They pushed and struggled over the jug.

Wade waited until the door of the house slammed shut. This was the time. He crept back around the corrals, careful not to disturb the horses. They were mostly Navajo paint-ponies, bony and undersized, yet of astounding stamina and as sour-tempered as Spanish mules. He came up behind the house, eased in close and prowled a lighted window. He looked into a fairly large room.

It was a room sparely furnished with a split-log table and rawhide chairs. The bare plank floor was unswept. At the front door the tramped-in dirt lay thick. The busted gambler sat at the table talking across an uncorked jug and two tin cups to another man, wagging his head and laughing. His face was the seamed and young-old type of his kind, bright-eyed, clownish.

The other man across the table had stiff white hair. His face was thin and red and sharp-nosed. He wore a faded blue Navajo shirt, wrapped around him without buttons. Max Luttrell, that one.

The window was shut. Wade couldn't hear a word. He slipped to the next window, which was partly open. He heard the busted gambler say, "... bunch. Never did like 'em ... any of their breed. I'm a white man. ..."

"Shut it off!"

Luttrell's elbows were on the table. His head had been bowed. He raised it and said further, "Drift on if you don't like my friends here. Who in hell are you?" He spoke with a lean Yankee accent, and Wade remembered that he was reputed to come of a good Eastern family.

The gambler, playing it low, said placatingly, "Now, Max, don't get sore. I'm just running off at the mouth, way I do all the time. It don't mean anything, Max."

"Well, shut it off." Max Luttrell stared blindly at the gambler. "I've done this five years. Six. I'm a Luttrell and I've got an Indian squaw. Who in hell are you?"

"Nobody. Just nobody." The down-at-heel gambler sloshed drinks clumsily from the jug. "Drink up."

"Nobody." Luttrell fumbled his tin cup up. He gazed far away. "I'm somebody. In the foul—no, fell—grasp of dire circ'mstances I have not winced. ... Ah, the hell with it. What were we arguing about?"

"Nothing, Max, not a thing," crooned the gambler. He refilled Luttrell's tin cup as soon as Luttrell clanked it down empty. "We was discussing the Indian problem."

"No problem there," Luttrell muttered. "Give them whiskey, you're all right. Take a girl like Ina. My squaw. No problem." He drained his cup and flung it over the table. "A drink, Sam."

"Henry," the gambler corrected, pouring. "Henry Torpe, me."

"Henry or Sam, what the hell?"

A girl shuffled softly into the room. She wore white buckskin leggings, and a colored blanket over her shoulders. Her glistening black hair was cut level just above her black, patient eyes.

The gambler said to her, " 'Lo, Ina. How's it upstairs?"

The Navajo girl gazed unreadably from him to Luttrell for a stolid moment. "She's a' right," she said in a low voice faintly tinged with truculence, and sat down in a rawhide chair away from the table, to the rear of Luttrell.

There was a tingling instant when Wade thought the brooding black gaze discovered him outside the window.

He tensed to run. But Ina sat passive, hands folded, seeming to be listening to the increasing noise raised by the drinking Indians in the yard.

He sank down, eased off and sent a stare to the lighted window on the second floor.

"*She's a' right.*"

It was a common term used in relation to practically any subject, from a repaired roof to the current price of beef. But it was not generally used by Navajos, and rarely by women unless indicating a person.

He estimated the distance up to the window. Too high to jump and climb without making some noise. He moved away and circled the house to the front. There an upstairs gallery overhung the one below. He tugged off his boots reluctantly, hating the risk of leaving his feet unshod. Still, it seemed less hazardous than the risk of hard heels scraping bare wood.

By stepping up on to the rail of the downstairs gallery, against the corner post, he could reach his hands to the floor of the gallery above. He pulled himself up and climbed over the railing onto the upstairs gallery. The sun-dried boards creaked under his weight, and he crouched listening. The Indians were raising more noise than ever, quarreling now over turns at the whiskey jug. That noise, though, could not cancel out any sharp sound within the house; not to alert ears. Max Luttrell and Henry Torpe were drunk, their senses dulled. But Ina was cold sober and Ina was an Indian.

Wade opened an unfastened window on the gallery and wormed through it. He felt on through a dark room to its door, crept out onto a short corridor, and sighted a crack of light to his right, away from the stairs and the reflected glow of a lamp below. At the light-rimmed door he felt for the iron latch, found it, thumbed it down. He pressed the door open swiftly, stepped into a bedroom and closed the door after him.

"Quiet!" he whispered to the girl in there.

CHAPTER 9

SHE WAS small, dark, pretty. The instant he opened the door, Wade recognized her as the girl in the picture he had studied so often, the missing girl he was hunting. No doubt about it, this was Louise Venning.

She had sprung up from the bed. She stared at him, frightened, cringing, backing away. Her heavy skirts were creased in the wrong places and untidily revealed an inch of petticoat on one side. But her hair showed careful combing in its upswept pile of fashionable Empress Eugénie crown, and her skin was immaculately clean. Nobody could mistake her for anything less than a lady.

But he had a terrified girl to deal with, and he had never found that quality blood made much difference when it came to fear. So he said kindly, "Miss Venning, I'm a friend. Don't be scared of me."

She stared wildly at him. "Who are you? I don't know you!"

He kept his tone hushed and gentle. "My name's Wade Forrest. I've come to take you home to your father."

"No!" She frantically shook her head. "No!"

He remembered. Feenix, the lawyer, had told him. She was strange, not quite right in her head. He choked off his angry and urgent impatience, and said to her, "Your father wants you back home. I'll take you back. Keep your voice down, Louise. Listen to me."

"No!" That frantic wildness still gripped her. She said rapidly, "He's not my father, he's my stepfather. My father's dead. My mother married again."

That was news. Feenix, the lawyer, had not spoken of it.

"All right, your stepfather," Wade said. "He wants you back and I'm here to take you."

"No!"

Her repetition dug at his nerves. He said more harshly than he meant, "Yes. That's my job."

"No!"

He fought down his exasperation. His set face mirrored

72

his temper for the girl to see, though, and she said, "My mother died last year. She left everything to me. But she named him—my stepfather, Eber Whitson—as my guardian 'til I'm twenty-one. Before my mother was a week in her grave he tried to come into my bedroom. I lived in horror of that beast for months. I thought I'd go mad."

He sat down on the edge of the bed and smoothed the top blanket intently, not seeing it. "So then you ran off with—somebody?"

"Yes."

She leaned tautly against the dresser, holding her hands folded, oddly like Ina in that motion of passive resistance. From Wade's gentle tone she found some release from fear, to the extent that she could close her eyes and expel a sigh and murmur, "He was kind to me and—and—"

"Chivalrous?" he suggested, knowing an old pattern.

Her lips breathed, "Yes," and Wade bowed his head so as not to see her face, for she was very young.

"We met in church."

In church. He considered it.

"I think he followed me in."

Yes, that was reasonable. A man would do that. Even to church.

"He followed us home. Eber Whitson, my stepfather, is a respected member of the church. Nobody would believe anything I said against him. Besides, he gave it out that I'd been acting strangely since my mother's death. People watched me, as if any minute I'd do something crazy. It was horrible. I was terribly lonely. I was afraid."

"I can imagine that," Wade said. "And then this man came along?"

"He was a stranger. He was passing through with another man, his ranch foreman. They were returning from taking a herd up the trail."

She paused. "He followed me everywhere I went for three days. We found ways to meet, to talk together."

Wade nodded, picturing the ardent lover brushing aside the petty obstacles, sweeping the girl off her feet. Arne Bassett could fill that part if his blood was up.

"He—he asked me to elope with him."

She fell silent. Wade asked softly, "And then?"

"Men are beasts!" she exclaimed passionately, and he had to flap a hand swiftly to caution her to hold her voice down. "We were married that evening at Villapoco, a tiny place up in the mountains. That night I found Arne was no better than Eber Whitson. A beast!"

Oh, Lord, he thought. She was a schoolgirl still. Her conception of love still ran to chivalrous prancings, delicate graces. He felt a half-amused sympathy for Arne, a man with all of a man's virile forwardness, who had let his redblooded masculine impulse carry him into marrying her. This girl hadn't waked up yet.

He said carefully to Louise, "Nobody knows you're married. I'm pretty sure your stepfather doesn't. He can't tap your cash and property without you there, so he wants you back. Is that it?"

"Or dead! By my mother's will it would all go to him then."

"I see."

He remembered Feenix, the lawyer, saying to him, "Find her and bring her back. Or bring back proof she's dead. Five thousand dollars to you, either way."

He began forming his picture of Eber Whitson, a man who, lacking the nerve for murder, possessed the necessary evil to attempt a shameful enslavery of a young girl for her inheritance. Eber Whitson had missed his object simply by underestimating the girl's desperate horror.

To that extent Arne Bassett won credit as Louise's rescuer. But the horror instilled in Louise by Eber Whitson had been Arne's defeat. All Arne had won was a young girl obsessed by vague Prince Charming fancies, a girl pitifully unequipped to be his or any full-grown man's wife.

From under lowered brows Wade studied Louise covertly. Her figure lacked nothing. She could incite a man to reckless lengths. She looked—he searched for the word and found a blunt and earthy one—ripe. And that, with her look of young innocence. . . .

He said, "Mrs. Bassett, he can't keep you hid here long. What's the answer?"

She stared astonished at his use of her married name.

"Why, he's promised me he'll find a way for us to get a quiet divorce. I've agreed to stay here with Luttrell. He picked up Luttrell, coming down, and they brought me here. He says our marriage and divorce must be kept secret. For business reasons. And because people would joke about it, Arne said. And he has a terrible temper."

"Yeah. But this is no place for a girl like you. This is no more than a renegade roost. Luttrell's an outlaw."

"Yes, I know. And that Torpe. And the Indians. Drunken beasts! But Ina takes good care of me. Somehow, I'm not afraid as long as Ina is here."

"I see," he said again, thinking of Arne's courtship of Beth, thinking then of Sheriff Stuart and Deac Shanter. Those two wise heads had shown in their different ways that they suspected Arne of being secretly entangled with a girl, this girl. What they hadn't yet guessed was that she was his wife. That was a potent piece of knowledge. Uncovered it meant Arne's finish. Beth, furious at his having courted her while he had a wife hidden away right on her property, would certainly give Deac Shanter the word to move against Gunsight. The range war that Stuart was trying to prevent would explode. Before the end everybody would be in it; for the nature of the Principe setup barred neutrality.

"Mrs. Bassett—" he began.

"Don't call me that!" she interrupted fiercely. "I refuse to be called by his name!"

"Sorry."

His apology was automatic, and on its heels came doubt. Refusal to acknowledge facts could indicate a habit of distorting them. This girl, after all, was not too level-headed. Her tangled emotions stumbled out of step with reality, skimming the edge of hysteria. She was not grown-up inside. Her story might be a patchwork of half-truths and fancies overlaying a bare structure of fact. Perhaps she had only imagined the evil character of her stepfather, had magnified acts of ordinary affection into attempts at sinister lust.

There may even have been no marriage, but merely the weaving of an old pattern. Then an intolerable weight of guilt, the refusal to bear it, and the defensive lies erected by an unsettled mind. She was morbidly sensitive, drawn too fine to support much strain.

Her small soft hands fluttered over her skirt, trying vainly and pathetically to smooth out the wrong creases. A deep and twisting pity for her overcame him. She seemed so like poor little Anna in some ways. Helpless and pitiful, making ineffectual attempts to cope with situations far beyond her resources. A lost little girl.

Out of his pity for her he reached and took her hands and said gently, "Louise, come with me. I'll take you home and I'll settle that matter for you."

Her eyes, after a startled widening, glistened, eager and grateful. "Oh, I wish— No, I can't. Not until he gets us the divorce. I won't stay married to him! I won't be his wife! I won't!"

He held her hands still. "And then what?"

She gazed blankly at him. She hadn't thought beyond that. Soon, though, she smiled. "Then you take me back home and—and settle everything for me."

He sighed for her. Lost little girl. So very much like Anna.

The door of the room swung in with such quiet unhurriedness it made no impress on his consciousness until it was half open. He pushed fast to his socked feet, gun drawn.

Ina paced in, noiseless in her high white Navajo moccasins, a stolid, chunky figure with black hair banged straight above expressionless black eyes and broad-cheeked face. She murmured directly to Wade, "You go. *Mi esposo—*"

"They coming, *señora?*"

The black eyes dipped in thanks for the title. *Si, señor.* They hear. They come. You carry her 'long. Is better."

Wade darted a glance at Louise. She shook her head, and he muttered, "Damn! Wish I could—"

No feet creaked the stairs. He caught a whispering and the dry snaps of rifle bolts. More than two. Luttrell and the gambler, then, had signaled the Indian men up to the house. They were drunk and all the more dangerous because of it. Their respect for peril would be dulled. They would not use the reasonable caution of sober men.

His escape to the front gallery was cut off. By the hushed sounds he judged they were topping the head of the stairs. He padded to the door. He blazed two shots along the short corridor, jumped back and slammed the door shut.

Tumult broke out in the corridor. Louise screamed. Ina went to her and circled an arm around her, crooning unintelligible words coined ages ago to quiet the terror of

Navajo children when raiding Apaches howled in the maize fields.

His two shots bought Wade the minute he needed to spring to the window and wrench it open. He scraped out over the sill until he hung by his fingers. The door of Louise's room crashed in as he let go.

The small gravel on the ground dug into the soles of his feet. He let his knees buckle and fell awkwardly, doubled over. Somebody at the corner of the house, on his right, loosed a shot at him. He rolled over and returned it. Bounding up and running, he heard the busted gambler shout, "Here, Max! He's out here!" Then another shot.

He dropped to a knee and slewed around. A figure that appeared to be all baggy frock-coat scuttled across a lighted window of the downstairs room. He fired at it. The figure hauled in, started back for cover, then tripped and became a floundering bundle. Max Luttrell, drunkenly unwary, framed himself at the upstairs window. He had a shotgun. Wade laid a shot at him.

Luttrell rocked out of the light, shouting something in a harsh, high voice. Ina began a wail, joined by another scream from Louise. The confusion of noises changed abruptly to a muffled rumble descending the stairs.

Wade raced across the yard. The stony ground dealt his feet brutal punishment. Damn, he thought bitterly, I might have known, leaving my boots, some bobble like this would crop up. There was worse to come, and no time to tear up his shirt and bind his feet before scrambling through Black Walls. The Navajo men were out after him.

It was nerve-tearing, the eerie silence of the hunt in the dark. After a few barking little cries they made no further sound. He guessed they had located the direction of his flight. The manhunt was clearing their senses. He was keeping out of their sight, though. They hadn't fired at him yet. In his frayed shreds of socks he could move as soundlessly as they.

Slipping along in the deep shadows of Black Walls, he thought he made out the hawk-nosed rock. It was not the one, he found, when he looked for the crevice. They all had changed, the great black shapes, thrown out of recognition by the shift of the moon and new shadows. A chill worm of fear rippled through him, transmuted the next instant into rage. He glared back at flitting shadows and cursed in a whisper and limped on.

The hawk-nosed rock, unmistakably the right one, loomed up before him. In sheer relief he snorted a laugh. He clambered up beside it hurriedly, gashing his feet on sharp-edged lava, onto the ledge of the crevice. There he lay quiet, listening. In a little while he heard the faint rustle of men creeping by below. When he was fairly sure that they had all gone past he crawled backward along the crevice, gun in hand.

CHAPTER 10

AROUND FOUR in the morning, at Glory Spring, Deac Shanter emerged fully dressed onto the front gallery, with a lantern, and inquired dryly, "Have you got so attached to my horse you don't want to get off? You been sitting there five minutes, cussing to yourself."

"Seems longer," Wade responded. "What do you do when your bare feet are stuck in the stirrups with blood?"

"I wear boots, except in bed."

"It's a good rule. But this time I'm caught barefoot."

Deac stepped forward with the lantern. He inspected both feet. "Damn if you're not," he commented. "These stirrups'll take some cleaning." Dried blood glued the cuts to the broad wooden stirrups encased in heavy leather *tapaderas*. "There's some coffee still warm on the fire. Wait, I'll get it." He went into the house and returned with a coffeepot. He poured the warm coffee over Wade's feet.

The bay horse registered some disapproval of such unusual goings-on, but was too tired to do more than shoot its ears and shiver.

Wade freed his soaked feet gingerly and said, "Guess you'll have to tend to the horse. I hate the thought of putting these feet on the ground."

"Horse can wait," Deac murmured. He put up his arm. "Slide off on me."

His strength was enormous. Wade was a big man, yet

Deac held him off the ground with that one arm, carrying the lantern, and got him into the house. He dropped Wade into a chair in the big room, set the lantern on the table, went to the cabinet and got whiskey. He filled two glasses and handed the bottle to Wade.

"Wash your feet with it. We'll get Doc Meek out in the morning." He lifted one of the glasses. "What happened?"

"Squatters at Circle 7," Wade said, bathing his feet with the whiskey. "Max Luttrell, another no-good named Torpe, and a pack of Navajo drunks." The sting of the whiskey in the cuts brought a wince. "And the girl—yeah, the girl I came here looking for. A bobble cropped up. I had to do some shooting."

"Who'd you shoot?"

"Luttrell and Torpe. Not sure about Luttrell, but I guess Torpe's gone, the way he fell."

"Stuart won't pull you in on that."

"No, guess not. No good, either of them." Wade regarded his feet. He thought a minute and said, "But she's alone there now, with just Ina—Luttrell's woman—and those drunks. Ina's all right, but those others—I'm not so sure. It worries me."

Deac asked curiously, "You gone on that girl?"

"Louise?" Wade shook his head slowly. "I don't think so. But I never know, any girl I meet. I'm not like most men, married or whatever. I've had to learn to be so damn careful—"

He snubbed it off, angry at himself for having gone that inch toward baring the wishful, hungry past.

"She's married," he said, "to Arne Bassett."

For once, Deac's eyes betrayed a glitter that shone through the calm mask. Then the habitual chill froze over it. Deac fired a fresh cigar. He remembered to pass Wade one, and he said, "You've had a busy night of it. So has Arne Bassett. Arne took Bar V tonight."

Wade sat up. "How could he do that? Stuart—"

"Stuart can't mend it," Deac said. "Frank Brouk tried to take Gunsight. Arne got the jump on him. In the showdown they tossed for who'd have High Folds. Arne won. That's Arne's story and he's got a paper to back it. Frank took a deep seat in his saddle, got a faraway look, and drifted. When I left Los Portales, Arne was prancing high about it. Beth was that much impressed she kept the party going for him." He rubbed his chin. "You say Arne married that girl? Really married her?"

Wade nodded. "Yes. And it's a bust. She wants a divorce. That suits Arne, if he can pull it on the quiet."

Saturnine humor tugged the corners of Deac's mouth down a fraction. "If! How're the feet?"

"Better, though I wouldn't say they're much good for walking. Or riding either."

Shanter left the room and came back with one of his white linen shirts. He tore it into broad strips.

"Wrap 'em up," he said. "We'll take the buckboard."

"We trav'ling somewhere?"

"To Los Portales. Have another drink."

Wade poured one. He thought it over and said, "What I had in mind was picking up some help here and going right back to Circle 7. If Arne's still at Los Portales when we get there, it means a showdown. I can't see how that would help Louise any."

"Likely," agreed Deac casually. "You're trouble-shooting now for T Anchor. That's my first concern. Do it up right, and *then* we'll call at Circle 7. If that deal doesn't meet your approval, I suggest you quit T Anchor and go play your own lone hand. Right at present you're on our payroll. On T Anchor time, let me remind you."

Binding up his feet, Wade gave his anger time to cool off. He wryly granted Deac's stand the merit of being at least consistent. Here again stood that cool and impersonal principle that placed T Anchor interests foremost. Such disregard of all other sentiment was, Wade supposed, the mark of a man in complete control of himself.

"So that's how it is, eh, Shanter?"

"That," said Deac Shanter kindly, helping him up out of the chair, "is how it's got to be."

CHAPTER 11

DEAC'S HAND, shaking him patiently, fetched Wade up from uneasy sleep. He was achingly tired and stiff and his feet were two lumps of pain. He had eaten nothing since last evening. His mouth was dry and his stomach growled miserably on the stale aftermath of the whiskey he had drunk at Glory Spring.

To his dull surprise the T Anchor buckboard was drawn up at the yard fence of Los Portales. He had slept most of the way from Glory Spring headquarters. Now he had to pull himself together, and with an effort recall why he and Deac were here at this gray hour of the morning. Only a few saddled horses were lined up at the fence, and no rigs except the buckboard. The party crowd was gone and with it all the music and noise, but the many lamps in the big house burned on in wasteful disregard of the dawn. The windows, glazed outside by the growing light of the morning sky, fought by the lamplight within, bleared an artificial sheen.

The saddled horses at the yard fence all bore on their rumps the connected dot and half-circle of the Gunsight brand. Deac ran a look at them. Wade, recovering a measure of wary awareness, did the same. Their eyes met.

Deac said easily, "Let's go in."

Some men on the gallery, huddled silently in the painted Mexican chairs around the little painted tables, rose to nod and murmur to Deac. They stared levelly at Wade, for they were Gunsight hands. Perse and Concho stayed standing. Wade split a look between them, and hobbled into the house with Deac.

The main room had the disorderly sadness of a roaring dance hall in the morning, littered with the relics of the nightlong party. A couple of weary Mexicans in crumpled white moved sluggishly about, picking up glasses, yawning. One at the food table had fallen asleep. A lone bartender stood steadfast at the drink table, arms folded and eyes closed. A serving girl whispered to him and he

81

sloshed something into two glasses, added water, and dismissed her with a wooden gesture. The girl nested the drinks on a massive silver tray and bore them to Beth Tarey and Arne Bassett.

They, Beth and Arne, sat at one of the small side tables, smiling across it at each other and holding hands. Beth's eyes glistened. Her face had a good deal of color. Like her father, she admired a winner. To win was the thing, the top badge of accomplishment, the standard by which a strong and daring man was weighed.

Arne was a winner. The sure knowledge of it lent him confidence. He had wrecked Frank Brouk in one stroke. High Folds was all his now. The Starvation Hills crowd would have to line up behind him. He couldn't lose.

Hell, he was set up to challenge the mighty T Anchor if he had to. He could even face down Deac Shanter. But he wouldn't have to do that. Beth was smiling to him, holding his hand. She was his and T Anchor would be his. To hell with Deac Shanter. He was a hired man. He could be fired.

Beth and Arne gazed dreamily around as Deac entered with Wade. Deac left Wade, strode to the drink table and, shaking his head at the glassy-eyed bartender and the serving girl, helped himself to bourbon. Glass in hand, he flicked a glance to Wade and to the side table, and sipped his drink. He drew forth a cigar, bit off its end. The girl struck a match and held it for him.

He murmured graciously, "*Gracias, bonita,*" and gave her a silver dollar.

The serving girl bowed to Deac. The bartender stiffened. Deac placed another silver dollar on the table. "You are tired, Epifornio, and I come very late," he murmured. There he used another courtesy. He never forgot a name and he pronounced it fully, giving it the Spanish richness and never abbreviating it.

Epifornio C. de Baca, descendant of *conquistadores,* bowed to Deac. "*Señor,* I am never tired for you."

"*Gracias,* Epifornio."

And, knowing the girl spoke good English and was proud of it, he added, "And thanks to you, Conchita."

He had them. He had them all. The *vaqueros* and punchers and such kin as they had around, black-topped and towheads. They adored his toughness, were proud of

him. He knew the people of his Southwest, be they Spanish or Anglo and he could handle them.

Wade, deserted by Deac, limped in from the door. Perse
and Concho Pace followed him in. Reese, Temple and the
rest of the Gunsight hands looked in through the open
gallery windows, measuring him narrowly. He had a feeling of loneliness. He remembered that his gun, stuck in
his belt, had just two loads left in it. He had not worn his
gunbelt last night to Beth's party, for that would have
been out of order, and he had spent four shots at Circle 7.

Arne Bassett stared at him, swiftly taking in his weary,
drawn face and bandaged feet. And Beth was recalling
that Wade had walked out on her for the second time last
night. The first time, at Toland's, could be attributed to
a drunken whim. The second offense was a deliberate
insult. Beth's jade-green eyes glinted.

There was no prospect of Arne's letting this occasion
pass. Events had made him big, a man of power with the
right to be consulted and heard on matters pertaining to
Principe range. He was no longer a relatively small
rancher forced to curry T Anchor favor. Possessing all
High Folds and the support of the Starvation Hills cowmen, he could count his Gunsight outfit as practically the
equal of T Anchor in strength.

To retain that status he would always need to think
and act big, be decisive, dangerous. He had the intelligence to realize it and the personal equipment to carry it
out. Any still unbeaten enemy had to be met head-on and
crushed at the first opportunity.

So Arne asked loudly for Wade to hear, "Beth are you
letting that tramp come in? It's not right, you know.
Others stay out 'til they're asked, like my boys. Give your
house a bad name, that woman-chasing drunk!"

It was too straight and raw to pass over. Wade did the
only thing left to him, even though it meant falling into a
bad setup. He moved over to the table and inclined his
head to Beth. "Sorry I had to leave your birthday party
last night."

She raised an irritated face. Her eyes were icicles.

"When did you leave, Mr.-er-Forester? Early?"

This was transparent, not subtle, not clever. Mischief
got into him. Suddenly he was himself, Wade Forrest, by

trade a trouble-shooter, alone as usual in a hostile environment, doing up a job for Feenix.

Deac Shanter, idling over a drink, had drawn out of it after steering him in. Arne was back in Beth's favor. Deac could not and would not side openly against Arne until that favor was rooted out.

"Yes, pretty early," Wade answered Beth. "I left to see about some nesters," he added, giving it purposely the tone of an implausible excuse. He moved on by Arne and faced around to Beth as if to tag something further onto his apology, and that placed him in position to watch the Gunsight men. He saw Perse and Concho relax. He had them believing that Deac had rounded him up to apologize to Beth.

Arne twisted on a smile for Beth and said contemptuously, "Some woman, of course. Catherine Larmor, you think, Beth? She came here with him last night, I noticed."

Wade shook his head. Rage, furious and urgent, washed up through him. He stemmed it and said directly to Arne, "No, I doubt if Miss Larmor's ever had occasion to go near Circle 7."

At the drink table Deac Shanter smiled faintly in approval.

Arne Bassett jerked up his head. A fearful black fury drove the contempt from his face. He made to speak, checked it, and whipped a look to Perse. But Deac, too, looked at Perse. Perse slowly removed his right hand from his holster, stepped back and bumped into Concho.

Seeing that, Wade stood still, making no move at his gun. Deac, then, would back him. That was what he had to know before going on with this thing, for he stood no shake against them all. In his gunman-gambler fashion Deac would see the play through, and in the showdown he would win or calmly toss his hand into the discard.

Wade raked a look over Perse and Concho and the Gunsight men at the front windows, and brought it back to Arne. He had to win this play with one card and tie Deac to his side, or he was a gone duck. Deac would not stay with a loser.

"No," Wade said to Arne, softly, "the girl I found there at Circle 7 was Mrs. Bassett. Your wife."

He had let it hang an instant too long. He knew it by Arne's settling expression. Arne had his defense ready.

"You're crazy," Arne said. "That's Louise."

Wade nodded, appalled by a sense of impending disaster "Louise Venning. The girl I came here for. You married her."

Arne laughed at him. "Why, you foggy booze-head, Louise is Perse's wife. Right, Perse? Tell him!"

"Sure I'll tell him." Perse came forward, glaring at Wade. "I've had to keep her hid on account of you—you skirt-huntin' scum! She's mine! My wife! Stay clear of her!"

Deac raised his glance from his glass and pinned it on Wade. Beth demanded impatiently, "What's all this? Perse, have you married some girl? I want to meet her. Bring her here. Tonight. We'll have another party."

Arne laughed again. "She's too young for your parties, Beth. I stood best man for Perse and we brought her down, and I never saw a shyer little thing in my life. We figured you wouldn't mind us putting her up at Circle 7, being T Anchor isn't using it. Perse, the ol' bull, he's scared to show her. Scared this wolf might steal her."

The blood of fury gushed upward in Wade, swelling his throat until his windpipe closed. It hammered at his temples and rushed into his eyes. He was almost blind with rage, but he managed to hold himself in somehow. Finally the haze lifted. His face still prickled with heat. He was sweating, but he could see.

Once again he could see Arne Bassett lolling in his chair at the same table with Beth Tarey, while Concho and Perse let hungry fingers hover near their holsters and Deac Shanter nursed his pat hand and eight Gunsight punchers rested elbows on the window sills ready to declare themselves in at a nod from Arne Bassett.

He had to get it across to Beth Tarey the hard way.

"Miss Tarey," he said, "will you please ask Bassett to move away from your table? His game's putting you in danger."

Arne Bassett stiffened. Beth stared at Wade, then turned to Arne. "Whatever is he talking about?" she demanded.

Wade said, "I'm trying to tell you he's rigging a murder."

Bassett came out of his chair, but he didn't hurry. "Beth," he announced with awesome protective dignity, "this tramp's trying to pick a gunfight in your presence."

Beth's lips parted. "Gunfight?" she repeated, green eyes measuring Wade. His expression made her recoil, and she sought aid from Deac. But Deac was watching Concho and Perse.

For a moment nobody said anything. Bassett edged away from the table. He had gone white but his heavy jaw was set. He had nerved himself, Wade knew. He checked Concho and Perse and Deac and the window-birds. He drew a long breath and made his play.

"About Louise," he said. "Bassett, you're a liar."

As the West's unforgivable fighting word left his mouth he slid sideways, hand streaking under his coat. Concho Pace drew faster than Perse, but his gun was still coming up when Shanter's shout of "Hold it!" blended with Beth Tarey's brief scream. He got his shot off, little Concho did. It roared and reverberated like a mine blast in the room. But the bullet came nowhere near Wade. It ploughed a splintery furrow in the floor and chunked into the wall. Concho Pace gave a high, girlish giggle, then froze.

Wade cleared the cotton from his throat and slowly tucked the .44 back inside his belt. He felt sick. Arne Bassett stood there with empty hands dangling at his sides, chalk-faced but smiling. Arne Bassett was developing fast. Arne hadn't even tried to draw. It took more than a smidgin of nerve to do that.

"It's gone sour," Deac Shanter said, apparently to no one in particular, but Wade understood what he meant.

"Y'see," he croaked at Beth Tarey, "your boy Bassett was afraid you'd end up believing the truth about Louise Venning being his wife. He was rigging it so his two gunnies—"

"I see," Beth Tarey said, and stopped to quell the soprano shrillness that shock had foisted upon her rich voice. She sat straight, regal, imperious, only the tense working of her throat tendons remaining to suggest that she had been woman-weak enough to scream. "I saw," she resumed, "that you drew your pistol in my home. I saw that Arne had loyal men to take care of you. Now will you please leave, Mr.-ah-Forester?"

Concho gave a whinny of protest. He still had his gun out, muzzle weaving, finger caressing the trigger.

"Put up your iron," Deac said softly. "I'll blast you to hell, you keep poking it around me."

Nobody could buck the T Anchor ramrod on T Anchor ground. Concho holstered his gun, darting ferret glances at Arne. Wade swiveled his head to catch Arne's signal: two fingers up and a pushing motion toward the Gunsight men at the nearest window. . . .

"Shanter," he said, but two faces disappeared before Deac whirled.

"Stay put, you," Deac barked at the rest, and they stayed put. But it didn't matter any more. Wade fought down a crazy urge to match Concho's giggle. He shifted his weight and his feet suddenly reminded him that he was a cripple. He listened for departing hoofbeats. There they went. He felt dead tired.

Beth Tarey was saying, "Get rid of him, Deac. I mean permanently." And Deac was nodding. Deac was tossing in that hand.

Deac eyed him as if they had never met before.

"Let's go, Forrest."

"Wait a minute," Arne said. "How long are you siding that piece of buzzard bait, Shanter?"

"Anybody leaves a stiff on T Anchor range," Deac said, "he answers to me. Get it?"

They went to the door, Wade wincing silently as he shuffled. On the porch, the Gunsight riders wheeled to watch them but none made a play. "I've only got two slugs left," Wade mumbled. Deac plucked at the front of his belt, keeping his back to the punchers on the gallery. His knuckles tapped Wade's. Wade opened his hand. Bullets dropped into his palm. Four bullets. They'd have to do.

Deac pulled up halfway across the yard.

"Those two," he said. "Temple and Reese. Not the bushwhacking type. They'll take you head on, somewhere outside T Anchor graze. If you're that dumb, stay on the trail."

Reception committee, very correct and honorable. Again Wade stifled an impulse to giggle.

"You're through here," Deac said. "Grab a horse and drift."

Wade said, "Thanks, I guess," and shuffled to the tie rail. All Gunsight horses. They'd be after him as a horse thief too. He picked a rangy, tough-looking buckskin, dragged himself up on the saddle by sheer arm power, and eased his feet into the stirrups. He loaded his .44, then whacked the buck on the rump with it. The outsized cob gave a lunge that made him groan.

They romped under the squared T Anchor cross-log at a gallop. Hitting the Miles Trail's pattern of ruts, the buckskin really stretched out, and Wade had trouble gripping the animal's alternately bunching, lengthening barrel with his thighs. All he could do was clutch the horn with one hand and let the leather pound his groin. It went on like that for half an hour.

When he tried to brace his feet in the stirrups, they tore moans out of him; and besides, the stirrup straps were too short for his length of shank and his knees stuck out so that he could not get enough clamp into his thighs. He went back to the cruel, limp-legged jouncing, and he ached from crotch to skull.

Stay off trail, hell. He could barely make it on trail.

He knew what that meant, and he told himself he didn't care. If they picked their spot in advance, he'd bull into it. If the buckskin overhauled them before they got set, he'd ride them down and let happen what had to happen. Even if they killed him.

The ascending loops slowed the horse. The upward cant of the saddle helped him hang steady, hand on the horn. He topped the last fold and halted to let the buckskin blow. T Anchor's graze shimmered, lush and green in the morning sun, behind him. Ahead lay danger, but he would stay on trail.

He nudged the buck into a slow trot. He saw a high rock up ahead.

They eased out from behind it, riding. They couldn't shoot half as well, riding, but they figured on having to chase him.

"Forrest!" Spud Temple shouted, and he knew that they were hoping he'd run. They didn't relish gunning him down, even for Arne Bassett. He sat the buckskin and waited. They walked their horses closer, and the horses side-stepped, swinging their flanks skittishly. "Forrest!" Spud called again. He wasn't liking it. He wanted Wade to make a break, to warm him up with a chase so he would feel right when he started shooting. Poor devil. Poor, dumb, obedient, murdering bastard, Temple.

They stopped at thirty yards. "Forrest!" Temple yelled, and his voice cracked. "We're comin' at you, man!"

Bill Reese said, "Shut up and circle him. He's—"

Wade slashed the loose reins across the buckskin's neck. The long, sinewy brute uncoiled, hurtling forward. Wade hugged its neck, braced for the crash. It didn't come. Temple and Reese swung aside, both blasting, ripping senseless holes in the air as their mounts sunfished wildly. Wade whacked the buck again and tore down trail. They had stopped shooting. They must have turned. He lay almost flat, leaning out over the buckskin's neck, and there was no lack of power in his thigh's grip now. He whipped a glance over his shoulder.

They were coming. They hadn't even lost much ground. They were fifty yards back, nice, distinct silhouettes against the skyline. He wrapped his legs tighter around the buck's barrel and jerked the reins mercilessly. The buck's neck bowed until he was almost biting his own chest. It broke stride, dug into the dust stiff-jointed and ploughed to a halt, snorting. Wade let the arch out of its neck and swung it around.

Temple and Reese loomed up, thundering, twice as big as life. Temple's wide, blue-shirted bulk was nearest. Wade's .44 bellowed and kicked twice, surprising him, as if it had a will of its own. Temple reeled as he pounded past, screening Reese. He made no sound as he slid sideways, and he didn't slide all the way. His foot twisted in the stirrup and then his horse dragged him, bumping and thrashing, limp and lifeless, as it spooked off the trail and into the gullies. The horse dragged Temple's body for perhaps fifty yards and then galloped off, squealing crazily. Wade quieted the buckskin and waited.

Reese disappeared from sight around the next steep curve before he wheeled, and he returned at a cautious trot. Reese was a cool one. He wouldn't waste shots until he got close. He probably intended to stop, too, before he began triggering.

All right, then.

Wade aimed at the horse. He clumped three shots at it and fought off a desire to use his last bullet. Reese's horse not only didn't falter; it catapulted ahead at a breakneck gallop. Wade slapped the buck's neck again, frantically. He had to get moving before Reese either closed the gap and crashed, or threw a fast stop and began firing. He was moving when it happened.

Reese reined in, and his horse kneeled.

The horse came down gradually, with an almost majestic dignity. Reese slanted forward with it, hanging on by instinct instead of jumping clear. He was still trying to right the dying horse when Wade brought the buckskin broadside. Wade saved his last bullet, but Reese let out a wordless, wavering, agonized yell and threw his gun hand across the sinking horse's withers. His sleeve snagged on the saddle horn. He fired aimlessly, twice, and then sank to the road with his roan pinning his leg.

Wade rode on, trying not to let the .44 drop out of his nerveless fingers. Reese's wild lead had torn through his gun arm inches above the elbow. His whole right side felt paralyzed.

Half a mile farther on, he wound his neckerchief around his arm, tying the ends of the tourniquet with left hand and teeth. And finally, guided by a wary part of his clouding mind, he pulled in at the south skirts of Maya and eased to the ground.

Mustn't let the Gunsight horse be seen. He laced the reins around the saddle horn and turned the buckskin loose, giving it a grateful send-off slap on the flank. It would drift back home to Gunsight and nobody would know where it had been.

He limped into Maya, wheezing, half crazed by pain, blood oozing through the tourniquet. Nobody was about at this sleepy hour of the morning. At East Street he surveyed the vacant fronts. A weakness overcame him. He reeled around to the back of the white two-storey house. He leaned heavily against the back door and knocked on it. And having got that far, he quit.

The door swung in and he fell in with it and sprawled on the kitchen floor. He lay there, a dirty shamble, his feet bound in soiled rags, blood splotching his shirt, mumbling, "Sorry to trouble you. I got no place else to go."

The last thing he heard was Katey saying, "Miss Catherine! Oh, Miss Catherine! You come right here quick!"

CHAPTER 12

Riding south with Perse, bound for Circle 7, Arne Bassett slumped in the saddle and gave himself over to bilious brooding. When you actually thought it out, everything that had happened was Beth Tarey's fault. His memory was reaching back again to that evening when Beth had turned him down. The scene was an old one, but it churned his insides every time he pictured it.

Beth had been indulging one of her contrary tempers. "Keep your hands off me, Arne," she said crossly. "Stone Age tactics may have been all very well in their time. I prefer a more civilized conduct. Frank will be here any minute, and I don't want to look mussed."

So Frank Brouk had arrived and caught him on his knees, behaving too ridiculously civilized. Frank and Beth couldn't refrain from laughing at him.

That was not to be borne. He went up the trail with a Gunsight herd sold on contract to a Wyoming feeder. He left the field to Frank rather than stay and be the butt of whispered jokes.

On the return trip with Perse he lay up in that Colorado town for a sullen Saturday drunk. He was not ordinarily a hard drinker. He was driven to it by the intolerable prospect of going back to the Principe, to defeat and the knowing grins. Perse stayed sober and got him to a hotel bed at the end of it.

Sunday morning, prowling the town in a fiercely restless spirit, he saw Louise.

She was fresh, young, and palpably innocent. She was such a clean contrast to his terrific bout that—as Perse cynically put it at the time—he got religion, of a sort. Perse then had no feelings about the affair, other than a relief that his employer had found something to lift him out of his black humor. Arne went all-out for Louise, thirsting for her like a man craving sweet cool water after desert heat and alkali.

It started untrimmed: the headlong pursuit of a virile

man for a desired girl. In three ardent days it culminated in an elopement, in a brief wedding ceremony at the mountain village of Villapoco, presided over by a mumbling old justice of the peace who repeatedly became confused because it was hard for him to draw his attention off the gold piece in Arne's hand.

In the three days between those two poles of happenstance Arne scorched a rapid road from desire to rationalization. Louise clearly was unattainable by less than marriage, so he would marry her. Taking her down with him to the Principe, as his bride, would absolve him from the stigma of his defeat there with Beth. He would parade this beautiful young wife around, and be envied by all men, not secretly snickered at.

Perse, dismayed, and opposed to marriage by reason of his miserly principles, stated the motive nakedly.

"Arne, you're just woman-wild, that's all. You're fixed on that girl an' to get her you'll swear to y'self north's south an' drouth makes the grass grow. In a week you'll groan an' wonder what got into you. I know!"

"Snub it," Arne told him. He was bright-eyed, feverishly active, drinking steadily. A glass in the morning before breakfast set him up. "You go buy that big buggy at the hay-an'-grain. That team, too. Here's the money. Have it set ready for the road. We pull out tonight. Ten o'clock."

He never doubted that Louise loved him. It healed his lacerated ego. As for Frank Brouk, if Frank got Beth to give her nod to move against Gunsight—well, Frank would have a fight on his hands. And Frank wouldn't have Deac Shanter, who wasn't likely to stay on at T Anchor and take orders from Frank.

A driving optimism possessed Arne then, uplifting him, giving him a rosy view of what had until then appeared a murky future. In his passion he saw his future through the stirring vision of Louise and his impending winning of her. In the time of his most desperate need she was the touchstone of success for him. He was overcome with his eagerness to take her and go on. Nothing could stop him.

But it didn't work out. Being what he was, a man rooted in a man's land, where self-centered ambition was the accepted rule, where fortune depended upon strong action and a readiness to violence when called for, Arne had never had the time nor the opportunity to cultivate women outside the limits of the dance halls and the shuttered houses.

You went after a woman and you got her or you didn't. It was that simple. Marriage was the price that a man paid for a "nice" girl. That tied up the thing, settled it to respectable conformity. It was what every man ought to do, sometime in his life.

It had never occurred to Arne that a man might marry a girl and yet not possess her. The hideous fiasco of his wedding night left him in an honestly bewildered rage.

He blamed it not at all on himself, but on Louise.

Hell's fire. Wasn't he her husband? Hadn't he married her, legal and proper, in that damned mountain village?

She must be crazy, carrying on that way. He had married a crazy crying girl.

The crowning irony met him at Los Portales. That was after he ensconced Louise at Circle 7 in Max Luttrell's care. He couldn't show off Louise; her revulsion against him was too plain. It would make him a laughing stock.

He went to Los Portales to see how he stood. Beth greeted him warmly, open-armed, after his absence. Frank Brouk, the stodgy fool, had bungled his chance. Beth was terribly glad to see Arne back. She gave a party for him, flirted with him.

He had to keep Louise hidden until he could arrange a secret divorce and smuggle her back home. The task presented fearful difficulties. In this sparsely populated strip of the Southwest, one's doings soon became public news. Circle 7 still belonged to T Anchor, and Deac Shanter had a way of learning about everything going on that concerned Tarey interests. Max Luttrell was a disreputable squaw man known to be trading whiskey to his pack of Navajo outcasts, and Sheriff Stuart had his eye on him.

Yet there had been no better place that he could think of as a temporary hide-out for Louise. Gunsight wouldn't do. A chance rider from the Starvations or elsewhere could drop in at any time, discover her there and talk of it.

The alternative of a hidden camp he rejected, from pride. Louise was his wife. It was decent and proper for her to be lodged in a house. He was able to disregard the peril to her from a drunken renegade and his degraded

gang, but his ego ruled against letting his wife be exposed
to sordid camp conditions.

He was in favor with Beth again, better than he had
ever been. He had to play it to the full, strike fast, before
Beth's wayward fancy lit somewhere else. To win her
meant winning the whole Principe. Security. Prestige.
Uncontested power. An authority greater even than Captain Simon Tarey had attained.

He had to get shed of Louise. Disclaim the crazy crying
girl, or lose everything. If Beth ever found out. . . !

He cursed Wade Forrest. What in hell was that tramp's
game? Why was he hunting Louise with such crazy-stub-
born persistence?

Arne had never heard of Feenix, the shady lawyer who
made a specialty of confidential commissions requiring
the use of tough, close-mouthed men. Of Eber Whitson,
Louise's stepfather, all Arne knew was what Louise had
told him during his whirlwind courtship of her, and he
had not been in a composed frame of mind to pay much
attention to that subject. He actually knew little about
Louise and her background, but from what he did know
he could reject any thought of Wade's being her former
sweetheart.

His worried puzzlement had begun as soon as he heard
the gossip of the stage drivers, the reports of the man's
southbound questing on the track of a small, dark, pretty
girl who had gone missing. Intelligence told him that
Wade Forrest was publishing his search purposely in the
hope of flushing out the man who had taken her; but the
challenge was more than he could ignore, and so, against
his better judgment, he had braced Wade on Toland's
gallery as soon as Wade arrived in Maya. He did it to
test the man, to find out his caliber. . . .

Well, he'd found out, all right, then and since. He wondered about Reese and Temple. They should have been
able to take him out for good, double-teaming like that.
But somehow he doubted it.

He wished he could have gone to Gunsight and waited
for Reese and Temple to report in. He wished . . . the hell
with it. He eyed Perse malevolently as they rode at the
steady gait, between a fast walk and a shuffling trot,
favored by cowmen when distance demanded a balance
against hurry.

"Halfway Perse," he snarled. "You sure bungled it, you an' Concho. You had him when he was drunk at Josefita's. You had him again at Beth's. Did you finish him? Huh! You an'—"

"Now listen, Arne!" Perse's brown-mottled face creased meanly. "You listen to me now. I backed you on that shuffle about Louise bein' my wife, an' I done it slick. You got to admit that. He just throwed me an' Concho off with that murder hullabaloo, same as he did you. He—"

"Ah, shut up." Arne spat early morning phlegm into the dust. But Perse was right, damn him. All he'd said before Josefita's was, throw a scare into this Forrest. And he'd left them on their own at Beth's. No, this was no time to cut loose at Perse. Forrest and that snake-blooded Shanter . . . they were the ones to fight, not old Perse. Perse had just been handy. It didn't help matters, bawling out Perse because he was handy.

But Louise . . . yes, Louise!

Arne wiped his lips. "Let's shake out of this goddamned crawl," he said, and quirted his horse into a fast trot.

Black Walls presented their huge, forbidding buttresses and pinnacles of chilled lava, erupted a million years ago and hardened to the consistency of glass. The brilliant morning sun could coax no reflecting spark from the sullen black lava. This was a patch of ancient death, as worn-out as the moon. The break in the dead-black dreariness could be discerned only by the traveled trail threading into it. That was the passage leading into the bowl of Circle 7 headquarters.

Arne and Perse entered the break, Arne raising a yell to inform watchers of their identity. That was the rule. Hail out as you rode in. Or likely get a bullet from the rifle of some half-drunken Indian sentry lying on a lava ledge overlooking the pass.

No thin call of recognition and assurance answered Arne's yell. Arne swapped a taut look with Perse, and they spurred their horses and rode in on the run. In the yard the Navajos lay in the abandoned positions of dead men around the cold remains of the fire. Not one of them stirred to challenge the two incoming riders. Arne and Perse glanced bitterly at them and pushed on to the house.

There Perse motioned down at another figure lying

alone on the ground: Torpe, face upturned to the bright morning sky.

"They *all* drunk?"

"He's not drunk. Look again."

"You're right," Perse muttered. "He's dead."

Arne sent Perse a stare of exasperated contempt for his superfluous comment. They dismounted and clattered quickly into the house. The main room, a boars' nest at best, presented a worse spectacle than usual. A cot in a corner had been overturned, and pieces of a broken jug littered the floor. The reek of raw whiskey was so powerful that Arne gagged and drew a sour mouth, his stomach queasy in the aftermath of his drinking at Beth's.

Some quiet movement scraped overhead. He stamped through the hog-dirty room and on up the stairs, Perse behind him. Ina came to the door of Louise's room as they stepped up onto the short corridor. Disregarding the Indian girl's brooding gaze on him, Arne shoved her aside impatiently and entered the room.

Max Luttrell lay in the bed, blankets drawn up to his chin. The face he turned to Arne was shockingly sunken, its redness bleached to cobwebs of brownish veins under a gray skin that was crumpled as though the structure beneath had partly collapsed. That, with his prematurely white hair, gave him the appearance of a sick old man. But he spoke in a normal voice.

"We had a visitor last night. Got Torpe. Got me. Got away." His colorless lips twisted spitefully. "Too bad you weren't here, Bassett." And, in sudden anger: "Why didn't you warn me? Damn your soul to Satan, look what he did to me!"

He flung the blankets down, which brought from Ina a low wail of protest. His body was naked except for bandages swathing his chest. The bandages were soaked and caked with dried blood, as was the bed under him.

Spending no more than a glance on him, Arne demanded of Ina brusquely, "The young lady, where is she?" Ina pointed with her chin, indicating the room on the other side of the corridor. Arne nodded.

"Why didn't your lousy Indians catch him?" he asked Luttrell. "Too drunk, like you?"

Luttrell let Ina draw the blankets back up and cover him. "They weren't so drunk," he said, "but he dodged them somehow. They hunted for him everywhere, half the night. That made them feel bad, naturally, so they slipped in downstairs and stole the rest of the whiskey. There was nobody to stop them. They won't be any good for a while, but later on Ina will get them to bury poor old Torpe. And," he added after a pause for breath, "me."

Arne shrugged.

Luttrell said, "He left his boots behind, whoever he was. He may have got himself lost in the Walls."

"He didn't," Arne snapped. "He turned up early this morning at Los Portales. Name's Forrest. Damn near queered me—thanks to you and your boozing bunch."

The wounded man began a retort, halted by a fit of coughing that shook the strength out of him. Ina bent over him and tucked her hand under the nape of his neck and raised him to an easier position, for he seemed to be strangling. Catching the wild glare in his eyes, she whispered to him soothingly in Navajo.

Arne paid Luttrell no further heed, but said to Perse, "You stick here today. Tonight, bring her to Beth's."

Perse's pale blue eyes rounded. He stuck a thumb in the direction of the room opposite. "Her?"

Arne nodded impatiently. "Your wife, remember? We've got to make that stand. I'll be there. I'll drop a rumor beforehand that she's not right in the head, in case she acts odd. You won't need to stay longer than just to introduce her to Beth as Mrs. Perse. Then you take her to Gunsight. That's all."

"An' then?"

"Then," Arne answered slowly, "we'll see. Maybe you could take her down to Mexico. I could join you later and arrange some kind of divorce there. We come back and you say you had to divorce her because you found out she was crazy. We'll work on it. Main thing now is to satisfy Beth that Louise is your wife and I got nothing to do with her. How about it?"

Perse shifted his eyes uncomfortably from Arne's straight stare. This was something far out of his line. He was capable of brutal violence to the limit and his morals made very light baggage. Elaborate trickery, though, was different. And this involved a woman. Two women, perhaps. There was a strict code protecting women in this Southwest country. You could kill a man and stand a fair shake of getting away with it, while even a discourtesy to a woman brought quick and unavoidable punishment. He wouldn't put it past Arne, Perse decided privately, to marry Beth before divorcing Louise, if Arne thought it necessary to move fast. And Beth was T Anchor. Beth was queen here in the Principe. She represented force: Deac Shanter and the great T Anchor hard-case crew.

Only a few weeks back Perse would have flatly refused, fearing what it might lead to. For that matter, he doubted that Arne then would have considered suggesting such a course. Arne then had been a pretty good and sound man. He had a wild flair, sure; but he respected law and the code of the country.

But in these past weeks Arne had progressed farther and farther along the tightrope of his gamble. And he, Perse, had gone much too far with Arne to turn back. Arne's success in breaking Frank Brouk and running him out and seizing all of High Folds, in a single night, had made of him a man ten times as big as he previously had been. To the high ambition driving him, Arne was committing every resource. He could not stop now.

"I guess I'll go through with it," Perse muttered. He appended hopefully, "I bet *she* won't!"

Arne's smile was as icily cruel an expression as Perse had ever seen on his dark, handsome face. And he had known Arne in many wicked humors.

"I bet she will," Arne said softly.

He walked out. The door to the room opposite across the corridor opened and closed quietly. Perse waited, wondering how far this thing must go, and if there ever would come a safe and secure end to it.

First, Perse heard Arne's voice. It was restrained. The words were muted and indistinguishable behind that closed door. The girl, Louise, said something, quickly: a negative reply. Arne talked on in that moderate tone.

The girl gave the same reply.

A slap. A cry. Another slap.

Perse sat down, crossed his legs, and trailed his pale glance to Ina.

This, he guessed, was likely to take some time.

The Indian girl wasn't bad looking. Probably would have a good shape, without those bundlesome skirts and clumsy leg-length moccasins. They often had at her age. H'm. . . .

Ina flinched, either at his look or the repeated sound of the slapping blows in the other room. In the bed, Luttrell moved restlessly and groaned an oath, either from pain or protest. Perse drifted his glance to him in idle curiosity. It was rumored that Luttrell was the cast-off of a notable Eastern family. Funny how the booze got these no-goods from back there.

Nothing more lowdown than a drunken squaw man, Perse figured.

Arne was speaking in a tinny, tight tone now, not loud but thinly savage. There was a sobbing tumble of words from the girl, and the slapping stopped. In a minute that door opened and closed, and Arne came in and looked at Perse. Arne's expression was about what it had been before, a smile that wasn't a smile. He said, "She'll go through with it."

"Uh." Perse stood up. "Well, I guess you know."

Arne looked down at the palm of his right hand. He stroked it with the thumb of his left. "Yes. Got to leave you now."

The sobbing, sunk now to a low, gasping rhythm, began getting on Perse's nerves. "What for?" he grumbled.

The stroking thumb stilled. Arne closed the fingers of his right hand and scraped their tips over the palm, making a dry sound; then he spread them once more, as if dismissing something, wiping it off. Also something had happened to his eyes. Perse felt much the same chill pricking of uneasiness, meeting them, that he always was conscious of when meeting Deac Shanter's stare.

"Forrest," Arne said. "Temple and Reese must be back at Gunsight now. If they got him, that's that. If they didn't, I clear what comes next with Stuart, in town."

He nodded and left. Perse noticed that his walk, too, was different. It resembled Shanter's walk, steady and unhurried and purposeful.

Perse looked at Ina, and rubbed the palm of his right hand.

CHAPTER 13

Loafing in his office on the corner of West Block, Sheriff Hugh Stuart swung his head from the match he was applying to a dead inch of cigar and watched Arne Bassett pull up outside his window. A quality in Arne's bearing caught deeply below the surface of his attention.

Thoughtfully, Stuart finished lighting the butt in his cigar holder. Long experience had equipped him with a full set of forecaster's tools for judging the weather of men's tempers. Here was a cyclone brewing. He sighed. Ambition too often became a fierce lust inflamed by each new triumph. He counted himself the better off for having discarded it years ago.

Arne Bassett's compactly built shape came up before the battered desk on which Stuart's feet rested. Stuart dropped the match on the floor, raised his head and said, " 'Lo, Arne."

Contrary to custom, Arne didn't take the only other chair, but stood there staring down at the Sheriff in an intent and assertive manner. The hard handsomeness of his dark, fiery face had grown sharper from the impress of something saturnine. It was a face that boldly bannered a spirit of reckless challenge.

It was that bad, then, the Sheriff mused tiredly. Well.

"Do anything for you, Arne?" He rolled a cigar over the desk to him. A politician's cigar.

Arne hung a glance on it, took it without thanks, fired it with considerable care. "I don't know."

He disliked the question. It tended to place him in the position of applicant, and he was here to lay down a demand.

Stuart, reading all that, murmured, "A talk, then. What about?" He pointed his cigar butt at the other chair.

Ignoring the invitation, Arne continued his inspection, and contempt knifed forward into his measuring stare.

For all his past record, what did Stuart amount to now? A small-town peace officer. A short and pudgy has-been

100

with fading old eyes, who never wore a gun and half the time couldn't find his badge. Aging, tired and shabby, rocking along on that worn-out old reputation.

"It's about that fellow Forrest," Arne responded curtly. "He's been trying to run a hooraw over on me ever since he came here."

"What you want me to do?" asked Stuart mildly.

"Nothing." Arne took a long drag at the gift cigar and threw it out into the street. "I'll stand no more of it. I'm going to get him. When I get him, I still expect you to do nothing."

"When'll that be?"

"Soon's I find him. And I think I know where."

Stuart nodded. He regarded his cocked feet on the desk, in their flat-heeled boots. "No," he said.

Arne's eyes narrowed. "Yes, I say!"

Plucking the burned-down butt from his holder, Stuart squashed it out on the desk. "No, it's a pers'nal quarrel with a woman at the bottom. All right, a lady, or ladies. We won't mention names. It won't justify a killing, in my book. I told Forrest so. Now I'm telling you, Arne."

"And I tell you I'm going to get him. Today."

The gaze Stuart raised was suddenly glacial and friendless. "Not in this town. I'll come after you."

"You'd never get me, Stuart."

Stuart considered that possibility. "If I thought so, Arne, I'd swear Deac Shanter in as my deputy. Deac'll pull with me any day. We have a private agreement. But I don't believe I'd need him. Look, I'm taking no side in this—"

"You sound like it," Arne rasped.

Stuart said patiently, "Look. If you and Forrest happen to meet somewhere way out on the range. If one of you afterwards comes in here and reports it was a fair fight, self-defense, and no witnesses to swear otherwise. All right. You'll find me broad-minded. Self-defense holds good. No jury in this country would ever convict either one of you, give you my word. But—" he tapped his cigar holder on the desk for emphasis—"no shoot-out here in town. I'll have no killing done in—wherever you figure he is. Remember that."

Arne's stare sparked and reflected the recklessly thinned margin of caution in his mind.

The Sheriff thought, *God, must it be?*, and slid his right hand with expert practice into the pocket of his baggy old coat. He was thankful when Arne's stare drained off and became withdrawn to contemplation of an alternative prospect.

Arne said, "I'll wait. But it better not drag too long. You better see to that." He stalked from the office. The Sheriff watched him leg into the saddle and hit the horse and take off outrageously fast south down the street.

Ending a brief train of thought, Stuart dragged his feet off the desk. He clumped them to the floor and stood up, sighing again. He tipped his old-fashioned round hat an inch forward, and, searching his vest for a match for a dead cigar, trudged outside and crossed over to East Street.

It was hardly necessary, he supposed, to enter Catherine Larmor's boarding house by the back door. There was scant merit of precaution to it, for Arne Bassett knew where Wade Forrest was most likely to be found. However, he chose it and went into the kitchen and said his hello to Katey, and sat down. Katey served him coffee from the ever-ready big pot on the stove, and he thanked her with absent-minded courtesy. She smiled, asking no questions, knowing quite well that something was wrong.

He had an unspoken partnership with Katey. Its subject was Catherine. Its object was to guard Catherine from her too-prompt trust and generosity. Failing that, they partnered in rescuing Catherine from the consequences.

It was odd, Stuart reflected, how much more easily nowadays he found himself growing attached to people. A peace officer, a good one, could not afford friendship. When he was young that had presented no problem. He had been able without much effort to be cold, hard, so neutral in emotion that he could arrest his own brother for murder.

Growing old and soft? He snorted at that. Old, well, yes. Soft he had never been and never could be. He had known this south-central New Mexico country when it was a notorious refuge for outlaws and renegades of the worst, most desperate kind. In doing his share toward bringing a reasonable measure of law and order into it he renounced the privileges of easy-going intimacy with his fellow men. The wanted badman could turn out to be the happy-go-lucky cowpuncher you had called friend last year.

Some silent call of thought from Katey brought Catherine into the kitchen. Smiling to Stuart, she seated herself by him and Katey brought another cup. She, too, knew immediately that something was wrong. Stuart detected the strain behind her smile. Women as well as men gave themselves away by tiny signs.

"Hello, Hugh. Thanks, Katey."

A womanly voice, soft. Stuart recalled his youth. A womanless and hard youth, ruled by gripping poverty and a blazing Scotch rebelliousness against all injustice. That was burned out, the young fire; now it was habit.

He asked Catherine kindly, "He's here, isn't he?"

Her hazel eyes were the clearest he had seen in a long time. They hid no guilt.

"Yes. How did you know?"

"Oh, guessed," he said, and wondered about those young years that had been his. He drew a breath and sipped the hot coffee. "He let you down at Beth Tarey's party that night, lady. Won't he let you down again?"

It was no use, he saw. She was young and full-blooded and reaching out to the future, not cautiously examining the past.

She said gravely, "But I know why he did that, Hugh. It was a nice thing. A compliment. He simply wouldn't let me take the risk of being talked about and—oh, you know what I mean."

"He pulled a whale of a drunk another night. That's not a good habit."

"Once doesn't make it a habit," said Katey sharply from the stove, and Stuart looked up at her in pained surprise, with a sense of being betrayed by a heretofore reliable ally.

"I know what made him do that, too," Catherine told him. She paused, gazing straight at him over her coffee cup, and asked, "Are you after him? I don't want to fight you, Hugh, but I won't let you take him."

"We!" Katey muttered.

Stuart shook his head. "No." Draining his cup, he got up, saying, "I only want to talk with him—" and there he hesitated to speak the fair girl's first name, all at once feeling self-conscious. Finally he omitted it, ending formally, "if you don't mind." He had called her Catherine, casually, for six years. A happy thing was gone. He would nevermore know it, he realized in his bare old wisdom, and he was going to miss it.

"Why, of course, Hugh." Catherine rose.

He followed her upstairs, went into the corner room with her, and remarked to Wade in the bed, "Hope you feel better than you look."

Wade rolled his head on the pillow, said, " 'Lo, there, Stuart," and groped swiftly under the blankets. His hand settled. He inquired politely then, "You want me?"

Stuart's irritated dissatisfaction came out on his face. "No," he replied shortly. "Bassett does. I warned him off."

"Thank you, sir."

The term of respect first warmed Stuart. Then it irritated him further, for nobody else used it to him and he sourly suspected irony. Catherine pushed forward a chair for him. He sat down, cuffed his hat back, and spoke bluntly.

"I told Bassett I'll have no shoot-out here. That goes for you, too. I'm taking no side and I want no thanks from anybody. Clear?"

Wade glanced at Catherine and back to Stuart, with complete comprehension. "Sure. But if he comes in here?"

Stuart said, "He won't. Presently he'll have a Gunsight man or two watching this house. He'll get you, or maybe you'll get him. But not here. Not anywhere here in Maya. I've told you both. It's got to be somewhere out on the range. I won't dig into that too deep, whichever way it comes out. Bassett says it better not be too long off. I think he means it."

"Wade's hurt," Catherine broke in hotly. "You're telling him to get out and fight all Gunsight, alone. That's murder!"

Stuart took off his hat, something he rarely did, and, cradling it in his hands between his knees, somberly regarded its stained lining. "Lady," he said gently, "that I can't help."

"Hugh!"

He went on half-frowning into his hat. "These two are vowed an' declared to a shoot-out. It's gone too far. I think I can keep it from happening here. What more can I do? I'm not too sure o' that, if—" he pointed his chin, Indian fashion, at Wade—"he stays here too long. Bassett's all fired up. I can't watch him night an' day. And a crime's not a crime till it's committed."

Some anger cracked through his tired restraint. He said with unaccustomed force to Catherine, "What else can you expect? He's took a rough edge to Bassett. He's kicked up trouble ever since he stepped off the south-bound stage at Toland's. Bassett's got way too big to leave him loose on the prod. Forrest, you know that. I don't have to tell you, do I?"

"He's after me," Wade conceded, "and I'm after him, I guess, soon as I'm able. I've got to, or run. Well?"

Stuart said, "You'll meet out on the range. He's gone mad-dog. I give him a day or two to hold back, no more. Oh, I'll go after him if he busts in here an' guns you in bed—but you'll be dead. Much good that'll do you. You better drift."

"Like this?" Wade asked. "My feet banged up and my arm in a sling?"

"That's your problem, not mine."

The cold statement aroused in Wade a flush of wrath, causing him to snap harshly, "Your problem is dodging trouble, seems to me. Well, I came here to kick up trouble. I'm still kicking. Is that clear?"

Stuart fitted his hat back on and stood up. "Sorry, lady," he murmured to Catherine, and shambled out.

CHAPTER 14

PERSE BECAME very bored at Circle 7. There was nothing to occupy him.

Nothing, until he got around to Ina.

He caught hold of Ina's bulky skirts as she passed his chair, and he told her, " 'Casion'ly I like a Injun gal. I kinda like you, *muchacha.*"

"*Gracias, señor,*" Ina responded tonelessly.

Like most Indians of the Southwest. Ina had a knowledge of three languages: her own Navajo, a fair amount of Spanish, and a barely adequate smattering of English. Perse knew the usual trade-talk of Mexican-Spanish, but for some time Ina and Max Luttrell had been whispering in Navajo. The chopped and strongly aspirated syllables were wholly unintelligible to Perse's ear.

Max Luttrell had never liked Arne Bassett, although he took pay from Arne for keeping Louise hidden and guarded at Circle 7. He detested cattlemen. In fact, the extent of his antipathy toward people of his own race in general depended upon how far they stood above his outcast state. Cattlemen behaved as though they considered themselves lords of the earth; and in his arrogant contempt of lower beings Bassett could hardly be outdone by any of them.

For the drink-sodden Navajo wrecks whom he had corrupted, Luttrell entertained a kind of faithless affection. The knowledge that he had dragged them down to their sorry level did not trouble him at all, for their main vice also was his. He had traded them out of everything they owned and could steal, for smuggled whiskey, then had gone broke supplying them with further whiskey on dubious credit because he could not refuse when they begged him.

The proposition from Bassett had come at a time of severe need for all of them.

Bassett's callously insulting treatment of him, now that he lay useless, fired his rage to the depths. For him it was a short step from dislike to hatred, and in that hatred he included Perse. So he talked to Ina in Navajo, which he had picked up from her, and ended by telling her where she might find a full flask.

Ina slapped her skirts loose from Perse's fingers and darted past out of his reach. Yet a hint of excited coquetry graced the flourish of her skirts, and at the open door, out of Luttrell's sight, she paused a bare instant to peep back over her shoulder at Perse before disappearing along the corridor and down the stairs.

Perse slid a glance to the bed. Luttrell lay very still, watching him. So. Well, it was damned little *he* could do about it. Perse rose from his chair, yawning and stretching, drifting to the door.

As if to change and relieve his position, Luttrell tried

to roll over on his side. The effort wrenched a gasp from him, and Perse eyed him sharply for a moment before going on out.

Luttrell sank back, whispering profanity. A poor chance, and it hadn't come anywhere near succeeding. Presently he got up the strength to turn himself over and work the loaded shotgun out from under the blood-soaked mattress. He pulled the shotgun under the blankets and lay trying to listen beyond the noisy rasping of his own breathing.

Ina padded quietly into the downstairs room, carrying a flat flask gotten from Torpe lying dead outside the house. She had found it, as Luttrell said she might, in a tail pocket of the gambler's tattered Prince Albert coat. Although given access to unlimited whiskey at all hours, Torpe had had to squirrel away a private and personal supply against the dread possibility of drouth.

Steadily meeting Perse's hot stare, she placed the flask on the table, moved a chair up, and motioned with brief eloquence. He grinned, watching her go into the kitchen and return with a tin mug. This was all right. Good little squaw. Knew how a white man should be treated. He sat down and reached to pull her onto his knees, but she backed off swiftly, the flutter of her hands saying, "Wait!" She put a finger to her lips and glanced coyly upward.

"Aw, hell with him," Perse muttered. "All finished 'cept for the shovelin'. C'mere!"

She fluttered her hands again, smiling a promise, and ran up the stairs. Gone, he guessed, to see if that boozy squaw man of hers was dead yet or asleep. As if it mattered a damn. Red, white, brown or whatever, women were all crazy.

His restless, impatient eyes came to rest on the flask. He was anything but an habitual drinker. It cost money. His drinking was limited to a technique of letting others—Gunsight hired hands, certain small Starvations cowmen seeking favor, and town tradesmen promoting good will—set the drinks up for him. His miserliness was notorious and somebody was always angling to trap him into standing a round, but from a score of tried and true tactics he invariably defeated their tricks.

This, a full flask, was free. He half-filled the tin mug,

drank it down in two gulps, pressed his thin lips and decided it wasn't the best whiskey he'd ever tasted. Injun stuff. Still, it cost him nothing. He poured a more generous measure. Thinking of Ina, he finished that and then another.

The symptom of a feeling of well-being crept over him faster than usual, and he gave it careful recognition. Better go easy on this stuff. Got a ticklish kind of job on hand tonight. Los Portales. Beth's.

Miss Tarey, wantcha t' meet m' wife.

Why, hell, he could carry it off. If she didn't pull some fool bobble, that girl upstairs. B'gahd, she better not. No, she wouldn't. Arne had tended to that, slapping her around. What they needed. Slap 'em around. Where in hell was that Injun wench?

He lunged to the stairs and yelled, "Hey, come down here!"

Ina answered obediently, "Yes."

It was all right. Plenty time before Beth's. Plenty left in the flask. He returned to his chair, nodding, and, finding the mug empty, moistened it, intending only a small sip to hold him till she came down. Somehow the mug filled right up. The stuff was free.

He drank that and still Ina was gone. His temper flared. He stamped to the stairs, swearing loudly. She was coming down. But he was angry at her and all at once contemptuous of her. He had something else in mind now.

"Gahdamn you, get her down here!" he shouted. "Bring her here! Yeah, her, m'wife, Mrs. Perse! Who she think she is? I'll show her!" He sloshed the mug full when he got back to the table, and sat down heavily. "Go get her, damn you!"

Ina vanished. There was talk upstairs. A door softly opened, closed. More talk. Feet descended the stairs timidly and Perse reared back in the chair and bellowed at Louise, "Get me somethin' to eat! I'm hungry!"

Narrow-eyed, he followed her with his gaze to the kitchen. Ina went after her, and Perse shouted, "Her, I said, not you!"

Ina explained hushedly, "She don' know how make fire. I show." She lifted the front of the iron cookstove. With a length of broken wagon-rod that served as the poker she hooked out ashes. Louise was staring wild-faced at nothing, terrified.

Perse emptied the flask. Dimly aware of a silence, he started up, mouthing thickly, "Cook me—"

Ina hit him hard on the head from behind, with the broken length of steel wagon-rod. She watched him lurch into the table and send it sliding, and paw at it blindly, and bump off onto the floor. His fingernails dug at the floor for a little while and then he went lax. She meditated hitting him again, but she was afraid to kill. She dropped the weapon and hurried Louise up the stairs.

Weakly, Luttrell asked Ina a question in Navajo, and she gave a grief response. He was dying, had been dying since last night, and her wailing was over. "Good," he said to her. "Good wife."

And to Louise, in English, "She'll put you on a horse. It won't be much of a steed and saddle. A Navajo pony. But good enough to get you to Maya. You go to the Sheriff. You can't miss his office, on the corner. Tell him—"

He coughed, and blood specked the blankets. "Tell the Sheriff everything. That," he said, baring a skeleton smile, "should fix up Mr. Bassett fine. Good-bye, madam. It's been a pleasure to know you."

Ina saddled a skinny pinto for Louise and saw her out of Circle 7, riding north away from Black Walls. She trotted back and shook awake the Navajo men and spoke urgently to them.

In a short time they rode out dazedly, taking along for burial the bodies of Luttrell and Torpe, tied across the backs of two docile ponies. There was some talk of appropriating Perse's good horse, but it bore the Gunsight brand and they decided against it.

When they had gone, Circle 7 became once more a deserted ranch, grass-blighted, worthless. It had never prospered for long, in any hands.

CHAPTER 15

W~ADE~ F~ORREST~, cursing savagely, was trying to straighten and tuck in the sheet that his nervous fidgeting had pulled from between the mattress and the footboard, when Sheriff Stuart pushed open the door of the corner bedroom.

"Took you long enough," Wade said. "How is she?"

"Catherine's got her quieted down," Stuart assured him. "How'd you know? Katey tell you?"

Wade nodded. Katey had come rushing upstairs half an hour ago, heaving with excitement. "That little gal you were after," Katey had panted, "that Louise whatever. She turned up at the Sheriff's office. Miss Catherine's gone over with him to bring the poor child back here." But that was all Katey had known.

"You tell me," Wade said. "I didn't hear enough."

"She rode in on an Indian pony, after sundown. I ran the pony off. Catherine an' me brought her here all covered over in Catherine's cloak. Like I said, she's calmed down, restin' in Catherine's room."

Wade sucked in his breath. For a moment he felt almost prayerfully relieved. But then anxiety rushed back into him.

"Bassett will hunt 'til he finds her," he said. "Then what?"

"Nobody knows she's in this house," the Sheriff said slowly, frowning.

"Can you keep anything secret in this town for long? When I bought that bracelet for Catherine, everybody —" Wade didn't bother to finish, for by his frown and his tone Stuart betrayed a lack of conviction.

He swung his legs out of the bed and sat up. "For God's sake, what does it take to move you? Nothing less than murder?"

Stuart's frown deepened. "Don't toss your horns at me," he retorted testily. "Far as I'm concerned this is still a woman thing, a fight between you an' Bassett over that girl. You tell me she's his wife. Where does that put you? What reason have I got to move in?"

Wade tested his bruised and cut feet on the floor. "All right. That girl's in a bad fix and so am I. Bassett's got too much staked to pull back now. I won't be idle when he comes at me, any time, any place. To hell with you and your law!"

"I know," said Stuart with startling gentleness. His faded eyes reflected the dark tragedies he had seen. "It's gone too far. You're both bound for a showdown. An' I'm bound to uphold the law, little as you may think of it. I cleaned up this town years ago, an' so help me I'll keep it clean!"

A masculine blare of voices lifted from somewhere below. Wade's cheeks slabbed flat and hard, and he slung out his left hand to his gunbelt hanging at the head of the bed, before halted by the thought: *No, it's not the tone.* A burst of laughter came in corroboration. Just some of Catherine's boarders, releasing tensions after a crisis at dominoes or checkers, unaware of the subsurface pressures concentrated upon this comfortable house on respectable East Street.

Wade brought his look back to Stuart, and interest rippled across his face. Stuart was withdrawing his hand from his coat pocket; the false alarm had started a prompt reaction in him, too. That pointed to a taut readiness, not quite in keeping with all he said.

"You're not as neutral as you'd like to think," Wade said.

"No?" Stuart went thoughtful, and paid out a careful reply. "As far as this house may be implicated, no, I'm not. Catherine won't get pulled into this thing any deeper than she already is, if I can help it."

"I see."

"Do you? How're those feet?"

Wade gingerly rested his weight from one to the other. "Well, I can stand on them."

"Then you can ride," said Stuart. His voice hardened. "It's a pity about your arm, but you're getting out of this house and out of Maya right now."

Wade raised his wounded right arm deliberately, and with that hand he managed stiffly to unhook his gunbelt from the headpost. Stuart froze dangerously still, eyes following every move. Wade got the belt buckled around his waist. He gazed down at it musingly. The gun hung in a right-hand holster and his right hand was not in shape to use it. He slid it around to his left side, which brought it butt-forward—an awkward hang for a left draw, but his best choice.

He said, "I agree with you about this house, about Catherine. I'm not taking orders from you, though."

Stuart stuck a cigar into his holder. He went through the motions of searching for a match, the search ending with his hand in the baggy coat pocket. So fortified, he remarked in a kindlier tone, "Believe me, I don't enjoy sending you on the dodge. But there's other things I'd like a lot less. You stand to set off a pile of trouble. You're the fuse on a powder keg an' I'm plucking you out. I see it as my job." With that much said, he added, "Sorry, son, but that's how it is."

Wade grinned pinchedly to cover his bleak loneliness. "I'm not figuring to make you ruin your coat, shooting through that pocket—but how would you go about running me off on the dodge?"

Sheriff Stuart twitched his shoulders. "Luttrell," he murmured, "an' Torpe. Two killings, by your own statement to me. An' maybe another accordin' to a rumor that leaked out o' Gunsight. Take me twenty minutes to get a warrant. You'd better be gone when I come back."

"I see."

Wade scrubbed his hand over his face. His long lips settled straight. He sat down on the bed and reached under it automatically for his boots. Remembering that he had left them at Circle 7, he swore quietly.

"I got a pair I can let you have," Stuart said.

"Thanks," he muttered, without irony. He stared down unseeingly at his feet, his thoughts indrawn and racing a despairing search. "How 'bout her—Louise?" And, the search pouncing on a possible track: "Wait! Stuart, listen!"

Stuart ducked his head to him. He removed his right hand from his coat pocket and found a match in his vest, knowing that the pistol would not be needed. Wade Forrest, he realized very well, was not afraid to shoot it out with him even under the handicap of a wounded arm; but the cause had to be adequate, had to have the balance of rightness. This was no run-of-the-road gunslinger with all his brains in his trigger-finger. The man faced doom, yet in his desolate extremity he still could call up a reasonableness.

"I'm listening," Stuart said. He was not so hard-worn as to be insensitive to tragedy. Rather, he fought to prevent tragedy from becoming catastrophe. To that he would be wholly implacable, while bearing sadness for one who must be sacrificed.

A fair recognition of the Sheriff's problem was expressed in Wade's ungrudging nod of thanks. "D'you reckon Bassett has learned yet about Louise breaking out of Circle 7?"

"No. I think he's dusting hard to Gunsight, to tell a couple of his men to get here in a hurry an' lay a watch on this house. I think that's where he went when he left me." Squinting through his cigar smoke at Wade, Stuart explained, "That's why I'm telling you to scoot now. It's your last chance. You might get up into the Freyes before they find you're gone. Tough tracking for them, if you stay close to rimrock."

"And tough riding for me." Wade shook his head. "Get me those boots, eh? And a buckboard from Wright's."

"Buckboard? Man, you can't get up over the mountains in any—"

Stuart broke off. Wade was shaking his head again.

"The Freyes can wait. I'm taking Louise. I'm taking her to Los Portales first, see?"

Stuart's eyes pinched to startled quarter-moons. He rapped, "Are you totally crazy? Don't you know you're all through here? I won't help you do any such damn thing!"

"I think you will."

They stared levelly into each other's eyes until Stuart gave in to irascible curiosity. "Name your reasons."

"Only one, and it's this. If Beth Tarey marries Bassett you'll have something more than a potshot range feud here."

Stuart made a turn to the window. "How so?" he asked, and came back around with a sharp, aroused glance for Wade's reply.

"Beth's bound to find out he's already married. She'll use T Anchor to wipe out him and Gunsight and everything else ever connected with him. You know she's got that much Tarey in her to do it and not give a damn."

"I know," Stuart assented, with a tinge of wryness. "I knew her father. My private opinion of the lady could lose me the next election. But I still got only your word for it that this girl here is Bassett's wife."

"You could write to Villapoco, where he married her," Wade suggested, "but that would take time. Better, you can hear her own story of it when she tells it to Beth tonight at Los Portales."

"Wouldn't it set Beth Tarey off on the warpath against Bassett, anyhow? Him courtin' her while—if, that is—he's married?"

"She'll be somewhat displeased at him, yeah. But nothing compared to what she'd be after a wedding. Think of it. Beth Tarey, queen of the Principe, made a fool of by a bigamist. That'd sure bring on murder an' massacre, wouldn't it? Lord! She'd wipe out Gunsight down to the grass roots an' go gunnin' for its friends!"

"I wonder," observed Stuart dryly, "how much you'd sorrow over a Gunsight wipe-out."

Wade lifted his left shoulder. "I could bear up."

There was a silence during which the Sheriff tugged out his half-pound of silver watch, shook it, put it to his ear, consulted the hands and moved to the door. Disarmingly, he said, "You got some other reason, I s'pose." Then crisply, "Some reason for wantin' to stop Bassett from marryin' Beth. What? Is it Beth?"

The question caught Wade outside of his habitual taciturn reserve. The answer lay buried too deep for simple presentation. He shaped a reply from the surface.

"Look, my stake is all snarled up in this thing. It's my job to take Louise back home. She won't go 'til she's positively and legally free from Bassett. It means five thousand dollars to me. More money than I've ever had at one time. That's all."

It didn't sound definite enough. He said again, putting emphasis into it, "That's all."

"That's all," Stuart echoed unbelievingly. "Okay." He started opening the door, but a further thought occurred. "If Bassett marries Beth, he'll have to do something about Louise—if she's his wife. Before or after. Soon."

"Damn soon."

"What?" Stuart spun around. They collided looks and both had the same thought.

Putting it into plain words, Wade said, "No, I don't think he'd kill her. I don't think he's gone that bad. God, what man would do that? Anyhow, she's not in that Circle 7 hole at Black Walls now. She's here in Maya. Your town. Here in this house with Catherine taking care of her. But —yeah, he'd have to do something soon."

"An' that's another reason or two," Stuart murmured obscurely. He went on out of the room, closing the door. He had committed himself to nothing. He would return with boots and a buckboard, or a warrant. He hadn't said which.

But it was a pair of boots that Stuart carried when he came back. They were old and scuffed, a pair laid aside as too worn for everyday wear, yet not worn-out enough to throw away. Stuart was not a prosperous man. His wealth lay in self-respect and prestige.

"Slit the tops down if they're tight."

He watched Wade's struggle with the boots. "Buckboard's out front. Catherine's gettin' Louise ready. Nobody spyin' the house so far, but you better get a move on."

Wade finished knifing the boots to fit and stood up. "You coming along? You can do the questioning there. That would put your official touch on it. After all, you're Sheriff. It's your right to find out who's responsible for a stray girl here. She could become a charge on this town, couldn't she?"

Standing with his back to the door, Stuart issued a tiny, cramped smile.

"You're sure tryin' hard. The town could stand it. No, man, this is all yours. You called for it. I'll sorta drift along later, maybe drop in at Beth's. I hear she might toss another party tonight, if the folks from the last one can crawl in. Better get going." He opened the door and waved Wade on out.

On the stairs Catherine said to Wade, "She's out there in the buckboard." The lamplight from the downstairs hall shone through the loose, soft, outer strands of her fair hair. She was always too busy the full day to remember to smooth her hair down, and toward night it fluffed out. Her figure, too, silhouetted against that light below, appeared more full than by day.

She spoke to him again. "Be very careful with her. She's very nervous. Shall I go with you? Please let me."

He shook his head, too conscious of Stuart back of him on the stairs. "No, thanks. You've done too much already. This trip's all mine." An edge of granite sarcasm made him add, "The Sheriff can make that clear. He knows."

She swung slowly around and preceded him down the stairs to the hall, and there let him pass her without another word.

His impression was that she was hurt or angry, that he had offended her. He was sorry. He wanted to say something more to her but Stuart pushed him on. The slashed, ill-fitting boots pained his feet, so that he had to venture each step tenderly in a straight course along the hall. Stuart hurried him.

And so out onto the white gallery. Down the front steps to the waiting buckboard where Louise sat huddled in a blanket, as shiveringly submissive and potentially explosive as a captive Comanche.

There, Stuart said to Wade in a sad drawl, "This once I guess I can afford to wish luck to a trouble-mucker. S'long, man!"

The buckboard pulled away. Sheriff Hugh Stuart stepped back to the porch, watching it swerve out onto the main street and Miles Trail, and thinking grievedly in the groove of tragedy so well-known to him, *There goes another one. But God, I like that crazy buzzard!*

CHAPTER 16

AMONG THE MANY baffling phenomena of this contrary Southwestern country, none was more puzzling to newcomers than the weather. Mares' tails in the sky foretold of storm, as any New Englander knew. Thunderheads meant coming thunder and rain. Not so, here.

Here, mares' tails and thunderheads could rear up and scrape the sky. Thunder could grumble over the mountains, and lightning slash the threatening blackness. And come to nothing. In an hour the sky could present a blandly innocent face clear of any hint of rain. This was dry country, semi-desert, almost a mile above sea level.

Thunderheads were piling up east over Starvation Hills. Wade scanned them briefly and knew they were false. There would be no rain. All the purpose those great black clouds served was to hide the rising moon. It wouldn't rain a drop.

He left it to the team to keep to the road in the dark. He held them to a walk, not wanting to barge into any other travelers who might be coming in from Gunsight. By now Arne Bassett had had more than enough time to send in a couple of his men, with orders to stand watch on Catherine's house, and their shortest route would bring them to the Calaveras ford and directly onto the stage road. Louise fortunately sat in huddled silence beside him on the buckboard seat, allowing him to send full hearing-attention ahead. Eyes were weak searchers in the clouded black night. Dwarf piñon and juniper were dark ghosts flanking the road, and white tufa rocks loomed up as gray sentinels visible only at twenty feet distance.

Barely a mile out of Maya, he caught a muted mutter of hoofs running up from the south to meet him. They were coming fast. He hauled on the lines, speaking quietly to the team, and pulled off. The buckboard's spindly wheels sank and dragged in sand, coming to a halt at a piñon clump. He sat listening, waiting, while tying the lines. Afterwards he drew his gun with his left hand and held it in his lap.

Louise must have seen his gun, although he tried to shield it with his coat, for she shivered violently. Except for that, she stayed silent and motionless beside him. She hadn't uttered a single word since leaving Catherine's house. Wade wished he could give her some word of reassurance, but this was not the time. It would take very little to send her into a fit of hysterics. She was too quiet.

Two riders hammered up, flashed by and were gone, riding hazardously fast through the black night. They pounded on toward Maya, shrank to distant drumming. Wade slapped the lines and pulled out onto the road. He hit the team to a spanking trot. Louise's continued silence troubled him, yet still he could find nothing to say to her. He drove at that good gait toward Los Portales, keeping his mind fixed on Beth.

Within two miles of his destination, he heard a rider in the rear. The rider swirled up alongside, calling out, "You an' the girl all right, Forrest?" It was Stuart, amazingly able with a horse, for his age.

"We're okay," Wade sang out. "What's the trouble now?"

They pulled up on the road. Stuart reined his horse alongside the buckboard, not neglecting to tip his old round hat to Louise.

"Concho Pace and another Gunsight man—Reese, you know him?—just rode in. Must've passed you."

"They did."

"Ah. They put their horses up at Wright's. They musta got it out o' him when I rented a buckboard. They were inquiring 'round when I left."

"*Muchas gracias, señor,*" Wade said. "So they're after me?"

"They sure are."

"And what'll you do?"

"Not a damn thing."

"No? Then why did you take all this trouble to ride after me? You could've gone to bed."

"I could've," Stuart admitted. He shifted his stoutish bulk uneasily in the saddle, never liking horseback travel any too well. "Oh, guess I'll hang 'round an' talk to 'em when they show up along about here."

"Thanks. I'd appreciate it."

"Now, I don't say I can turn 'em back. It's a free road. And a crime—"

"Isn't a crime 'til it's committed," Wade finished for him. "Yeah, so I've heard. But if you'll stall 'em, well, thanks."

He slap-reined the team and the buckboard rolled on.

All the lights shone at Los Portales, but party-noise was absent and would be for another hour, and the yard fence held no tied horses or rigs. For the working people of Principe this was roundup time. They worked from can't to can't—from can't see in the early morning to can't see at night—and then they had to wash and shave, or prink up their hair, and get dressed and ride ten to twenty miles. At roundup time a party didn't get off to a really good start until about midnight. It went off like a fire-cracker then until five in the morning, when everybody went back to work. Sleep could be laid up 'til next winter, they said.

Wade got down and tied up at the fence. He found Louise to be as docile as a sleepwalker when he handed her down from the buckboard. Music met them as they approached the lantern-hung portico, coming from Beth's foreign-made grand piano, the only one between Denver and El Paso; it had cost a fabulous sum to freight. For some reason the music halted Louise. In the light from the portico her face showed as a blank mask, while emotion of some kind worked in her wide-open eyes. Wade noticed for the first time that her cheeks were puffed and had a bad color, as if bruised. He urged her gently on into the house. He was deeply sorry for her, but felt that this offered the only possible solution to her strange predicament. Make known the facts. Make Bassett do the right and straightforward thing, free her and be done with it. That would break a situation whose course was leading directly to bigamy, murder, and an all-out range war.

The grand piano stood in an alcove built especially for it off the big main room. The music room, that alcove was called. Its shelves held nothing but sheet music, captioned exotically in Italian, French, German, mostly bound in fine leather that no cowman was able to recognize. Guests shied clear of that alcove.

Beth was playing something, a French-sounding tune, tinkly and softly romantic. She turned her head, smiling, to see who had come in. Her dress tonight was of an intermediate shade of coppery red that few women could dare to wear unless gifted with her natural accessories of jade-green eyes and bright chestnut hair. The low-cut bodice framed proud billows, and the creamy smoothness of her skin spread up without flaw to her white neck and delicately rouged face; for she never allowed sun and weather to meddle with her complexion. She was as conscious of her lavish share of beauty as a banker of his capital, and as candidly concerned with making the most of it.

A man's woman at all times, she sparkled feminine eyes incorrigibly at first sight of Wade, before swift recollection smothered that reaction. Her cooled look swept over

Louise and back to the piano, and she let them stand waiting until the piece she played reached its end.

Rising then with the resigned graciousness of a mistress bothered by unwanted callers, she inquired, "You wish to see . . . ?" Obviously, her tone implied, they sought somebody among the hired help, and should have gone around to the back.

"Wish to see *you*," Wade murmured, not trying to conceal his amusement. "Wish you to meet Mrs. Bassett." To Louise he said in a different tone, "Mrs. Bassett, Miss Tarey."

His eyes were on Beth's face. It took him a few seconds to realize that Louise had shaken her head and shrunk back in automatic protest. He dipped a close look at her beside him, his sureness suddenly betrayed, remembering her illogically frantic refusal, at Circle 7, to be called by her married name. Remembering, too, how it had then aroused in him some doubt of her bizarre story.

She still wore that same heavy dress, wrinkled and dusty; she was too small for anything of Catherine's to fit her and there had been no time to make changes. And, miserably abashed in the presence of the resplendently gowned and groomed Beth, she was fluttering her hands over her skirt again in that pitifully impossible attempt to smooth it out. She could not face unpleasant facts, and her unreliable nerves were in far worse state than when Wade had talked with her at Circle 7. Wade wondered if her puffed and discolored cheeks had anything to do with it. He raised his glance to Beth.

If Beth could have seen Louise at her best, Wade guessed, she might have listened with a mind at least partly open. She would have seen a small, dark, pretty girl, and probably she had few illusions about Bassett as a man. But, inspecting Louise now for the first time, all she saw was a dowdy mouse with a wan face, bad color, and hair as untidy as her dress.

"Poor little thing," she said in a voice of real pity. "I'll get you a drink presently, but first—"

She crossed the big room, away from them. She opened a door there and called through, "Epifornio! *S'il vous plaît*—I mean, *por favor*—ask Mr. Bassett to come here at once if he is dressed."

Those casual words punched a shock through Wade.

He heard Louise mouth a sound and he whirled after her. Pain knifed his feet at his rough use of them, but he caught Louise out on the front gallery and held her.

"You can't run off in the dark, girl. You'll get lost. It's five miles to town!"

Strangely, she didn't struggle at all. As soon as his hold fell on her she crouched, whimpering. He couldn't stand it. Her terror bent him toward taking her to the buckboard, taking her back to Catherine's. He pulled her to her feet, thinking fast.

Bassett must have ridden over from Gunsight immediately after he'd dispatched Concho and Reese into Maya to stake out Catherine's house. Why the haste? He couldn't guess. But anyhow, Beth apparently had let Arne wash up here, and he might ruin everything. Then again, confronted by Louise . . .

A rider hammered up Miles Trail from the south, swung in and came bobbing at the fence in the dark: a man in a mad hurry.

Wade put his arm around Louise. He whispered to her, "It's all right. You won't be hurt here. Beth won't let him hurt you. It's better we go back in." He sent a follow-up look at that rider from the south. The man bowed forward in his saddle and crawled off unsteadily. He was drunk or hurt. He dragged a carbine from the saddle-scabbard and groped along the fence to the gate.

Some other riders were sending the soft beat of their coming down from the north. Beth's latest party was due to get off to a start pretty soon. Her parties were never dull, never unattended even by the most stiffly conservative folks of the Principe. Beth Tarey *was* the Principe— or had been until Arne Bassett took over all High Folds on the east side and grew big by right of conquest and the compulsory backing of his Starvation Hills neighbors.

Arne Bassett was asking, "What is it, Beth?" when Wade drew Louise back into the brilliantly lighted house.

Bassett failed to see them right away. His back was to the front door. He was speaking to Beth, who had taken her seat at the grand piano. So Beth waved a hand and said serenely, "Arne, dear, meet your wife—so Mr. Forrest tells me!"

She got the name right that time.

CHAPTER 17

ADMIRABLE SELF-CONTROL laid a deliberateness upon Arne Bassett's manner of wheeling slowly around. It may have sprung from cold shock, but his poise matched that of Beth, who patted his arm, saying, "Congratulations. Can she cook?"

Arne raked Wade and Louise with an expressionless stare, but spoke to Beth. "I don't think this is funny. Nor is it going to be."

His dark hair, usually in crisp order, bushed uncombed and wet, and he wore no coat or necktie. In spite of that, his domineering assurance protruded, more pronounced than ever. What had been fiery impulsiveness, dash, cocky elegance, had vitrified to a solid iron of resolution.

"*My* wife?" His voice measured out a mild amount of annoyed puzzlement. Sustained by Beth's obvious disbelief of the claim, he snapped harshly, as any man might who was the victim of a bad joke, "Forrest, are you crazy or is she? I ought to kill you!"

Wade said, "I look for you to try it. Yourself, I hope. Not your crew."

They could all hear the uncertain plodding, the boot-crunch of a man navigating from the fence toward the lighted house. The two-hours-after-sundown breeze had not yet arrived from the desert below Black Walls. The night outside still hung quiet, and here inside this mammoth house, too, quietness persisted.

Beth murmured something.

Wade didn't hear what Beth said. Arne Bassett did, and he switched his forthright stare from Wade to Louise and demanded of her in the same harsh voice, "Whose wife are you? Tell the truth! Who's your husband?"

He began slapping his right hand on his thigh, his eyes fastened on her. The girl cringed, watching that hand. She was petrified. She made no sound.

The hideously brutal significance of Bassett's slapping

hand, of Louise's puffed cheeks, slit like lightning. Wade said flatly, "You dirty snake."

His left hand emptied the awkward back-to-front holster as swiftly as he had ever drawn from the natural right. The muzzle covered Arne Bassett and the hammer was cocked.

Whistling a breath through his nose, Arne said, "I'm not carrying a gun, you notice." His daredevil recklessness erupted through the newly acquired layer of austerely settled authority. "Go on an' shoot, damn your soul. Hang for it!"

Beth, talking in a shrill voice, was a disregarded source of minor sound. Equally forgotten, Louise crouched to her knees and shivered, hands over her ears, eyes shut tight.

The stumbling man reeled into the room, clutching at any object promising support. He was Perse. His mottled face presented a background of very sick gray spotted with brownish blotches and streaked down by dried rivulets of blood from an ugly gash that matted the hair of his scalp. Perse was in a bad way: a hangover and a conk on the head.

He peered sorrowfully at Arne Bassett.

Even in this country, where your neighbor could be a tired old lobo from the dim trails of the owl-hoot brethren, yet you called him friend, the relationship between Arne Bassett and his Gunsight foreman, Colin Perse, gave rise constantly to speculation. Perse's loyalty to Bassett was unquestioned. Perse would go to hell for Bassett and bring him back the devil's pitchfork. Bassett had a good foreman there. He must have pulled Perse out of a bad scrape at some time, folks said. Somehow he had won Perse to him.

They didn't know Perse. The soured, miserly man had been an outcast all his life, separated from other men because he hated them, hated their free-spending comradeship in which he could never join. In Arne Bassett he sensed a passion that he understood, *simpático* with his own—the driving desire to be above other men. The thought and the vision blended, hardened. He would back Bassett to the last chip.

Perse was the man Arne had ridden over here to inter-

cept. He hadn't trusted slow-minded Perse to introduce
Louise as his wife without bobbling.

Arne stared back at him narrowly.

"Put that carbine down," Wade said to Perse.

Arne rapped out a countermand. "Don't do it!"

There was silence and a creeping tension, during which
Perse slid his pale, sick eyes to Wade's gun. He was carrying the carbine in his right hand, at its point of balance
ahead of the trigger guard. To bring it up for use would
entail radical motion, more risk than most men in their
senses would care to take on against a drawn and cocked
pistol.

Wade brought the .44 around to bear on him, leaving
Arne uncovered. And still it was a toss-up what Perse
would do. The man was half crazed and wholly unpredictable.

A movement from Arne caught in the outer edge of
Wade's field of vision, and he flicked him a rapid glance.
Arne had a hand raised in signal to Perse, plainly meaning, "Wait, hold it." Now the riders from the north were
trotting down close. Judging from the altering sound of
the hoofbeats, they were turning off at the house.

The upshot was that Perse did nothing but hold onto
his carbine and wait for a likelier opportunity. Arne beck-
oned to him, after saying something to Beth, and crossed
to the drink table, remarking, "Colin, you look as if you
need a drink."

Passing Louise, Perse pinned a dull glare on her and
made as if to speak, but Arne called imperatively, "Come
on, come on!" He shambled on to the table, where he
stood guiltily avoiding Arne's eyes.

Saddles creaked faintly under the shifting weight of
dismounting riders at the fence, and in a moment the men
could be heard walking into the yard. They were unusually reticent for party arrivals. Wade touched Louise. She
partly straightened up in response, but kept her head
bowed like a painfully shy child hiding its face in company.

Arne poured a stout four fingers of whiskey into a
tumbler for Perse. "What the hell happened to you?" he
whispered.

"She got behind me with a kitchen poker," Perse whispered hoarsely. He drank half the whiskey and shuddered. "Damn near brained me!"

"*She* did?"

"Nobody else would of had any cause to hit me, would they?"

"What was she doing downstairs—" Arne began, and was stopped by the trampling of the men on the front portico.

It was a strangely ambiguous scene that Sheriff Stuart walked into. Perse, bloody-headed, was apparently having a friendly drink with his boss, Arne Bassett, who for once wasn't fully dressed. Beth Tarey, across the room from them, leaned pensively on the grand piano in the attitude of one waiting for somebody to ask her to play. Louise stood bowed like a condemned culprit. Wade Forrest was uncocking his gun. Not one of them said a word.

Concho and Reese followed Stuart as far as the open door, but didn't come in. Stuart pushed his hat back, hung his thumbs in the bottom pockets of his vest, looked everything over twice and finally commented, "Beth, that dress is a minute from immorality."

She inclined her head. "Thank you, kind sir. I'm twice happy to see you. There's a situation here."

Raising an eyebrow, he gazed at Perse. "Anybody been hurt?" he asked blandly.

Perse began a snarled retort. Arne struck him on the arm and said, coming forward, "Don't talk so smart, Stuart. It's not funny. Forrest slugged Perse today and stole his wife. He brought her here tonight and tried to tell Beth, by God, that she's *my* wife! He didn't know I was here. Perse showed up and would've killed him—nobody could blame him, either—only Forrest had his gun out."

It was glib, plausible, and intended chiefly for Beth. Wade kept silent, waiting for Stuart to make mention of a contrary fact or two known to him.

"Well, well," Stuart murmured, wagging his head at Wade. "You *are* one heller!" He ambled aimlessly off, stopped to look at a painting on the wall, and swung around with an air of having come to a decision.

Concho and Reese, at the door, were watching Wade alertly. Perse had changed hold on his carbine. Stuart said, "Look, Arne, don't take it that I'd throw doubt on you an' Perse."

"No?" Arne's tone caused Concho and Reese to glance at him and transfer half their attention to the Sheriff. Perse quickly finished his whiskey and nursed his carbine in both hands.

"All we want here," pursued Stuart, "is the truth. Ain't that so, Arne? Seems to me the young lady could put in a word an' clinch it for you. She knows whose wife she is, don't she, an' what it was happened today? Fact is, she's the party mostly concerned. Right?"

Arne said over his shoulder to Beth, moderately, "Why, I guess he's right on that, eh? Yes, of course, Stuart. Ask her."

Stuart nodded and peered at Louise. "Young lady." He waited for her to look his way and he inquired bluntly, "Is Mr. Bassett your husband?"

Wade held his breath, watching her, straining to help her and give her the courage to speak out. Her pale little face worked, twitched, and her lips opened, but no sound came.

The slap of Arne's hand on his thigh, a seemingly impatient gesture, did the work of a gunshot.

She gasped, "I—I—" and her features seemed to dissolve. She shook her head wildly. She screamed and crumpled. Wade caught her before her face could hit the floor. She was limp. Stuart helped him get her to a couch.

Beth said, "God, the poor little thing," and dragged a Navajo blanket from another couch and came with it. "Arne, get her a drink."

Wade and Stuart looked at each other. In Stuart's faded eyes lurked deep disappointment.

Arne brought a full glass of whiskey to Beth. Beth snapped, "One drink, I said. Want to kill the poor child?" She swallowed some of it, then bent over Louise and raised the girl's head.

Arne walked back to the drink table. He put a scrutiny on Perse, on Concho and Reese. He brought it to Stuart and said "No more doubts? Then good-bye, Sheriff. We'll take care of your friend Forrest."

"Now, Arne, let's not have trouble."

"No trouble at all, Sheriff. I'm going to see that lecher run out an' fixed for good. I've got cause. So's Perse.

There ain't a damn thing you'll do about it—unless you're siding a gunslinging, woman-chasing drunk against those who keep you in office an' pay your wages."

Stuart suddenly barked, "Concho, Reese, keep your hands clean. Perse, ground your carbine—down with it men!" Then to Arne Bassett, deliberately, "I'm taking Forrest in on two murder charges. Luttrell an' Torpe. He's my prisoner an' I never lost one yet. Forrest, hand over your gun. You're under arrest.

Wade slowly gave it, butt foremost. Stuart took it and held it in his left hand. His right hand had slipped into his coat pocket, somehow, without notice. Because he had to, he was shedding his comfortable role of an easygoing, slovenly Sheriff in an average cow town. He was the law-man who, in his day, had trod a path of tall reputation. He was showing them.

Arne flared, "Stuart, you can't run that over on me. Perse has got every right to gun him. He took Perse's wife!"

Stuart stared him out. "A word from Villapoco will clear up whose wife she is. The lady's feather-headed, and besides that's outside my concern. I'm taking Forrest in, I ask you—" Stuart's glance encompassed, in a sweep, Arne, Perse and Concho and Reese—"not to interfere. Please," he added gently.

From some old wisdom, some sign of abatement of reckless purpose, he must have known the time was ripe. He turned casually to Wade, superbly indifferent to Perse's carbine, and said, "Leg ahead out. An' don't forget I'm right behind you."

At the front door Concho and Reese split to let them pass. They paced down through the yard, and at the gate Stuart said, "Climb in your buckboard an' line for town. I'm still behind you. Don't pull out till I get on my horse."

With the reins of the buckboard team in his hands, Wade called back quietly, "How 'bout letting me have my gun? I feel kind of naked."

Stuart mounted and circled his horse alongside the buckboard.

"Start getting used to it," he said. "Court don't con-vene 'til next October."

Arne Bassett swung back from the door after listening

to Wade and Stuart start off. He darted a glance at the couch. Louise was sitting up weakly, coughing because of the whiskey. Patting her shoulder, Beth stated with hushed sickroom positiveness, "There, dear, you're fine." Beth had never fainted in her life.

At the drink table, Perse helped himself liberally. Concho and Reese were edging farther into the room, watching him pour and drink. They thought the problem of Wade and Stuart was solved. Arne nodded and hooked a thumb at the table, and they practically ran to it.

Arne walked behind the couch. "Beth, dear, don't you think Perse better take her home?" he suggested. "Can't have her here when the folks come, you know. She's—well, you can't tell what she might do."

Beth seemed dubious. But Louise started violently at the voice behind her, making erratic motions with her hands. Beth sighed helplessly and nodded. "I suppose you're right."

"Mind if he borrows your buggy?"

"Of course not. The poor girl can't ride like this."

"You've got a heart of gold, Beth," Arne murmured softly.

In a far different voice he snapped at Perse, "Put that bottle down and get your wife home." And to Concho and Reese, "Give him a hand with her, then team up Miss Tarey's buggy. Come on, get her out to fresh air—quick!"

They bore Louise out to the front portico. She fainted off again. Reese blurted something about it. Arne hit him a back-hand blow in the belly to shut him up. Then he said to Perse, "Don't let her loose to come here again, damn you. This time, take care of her right!"

Concho and Reese raised startled eyes at his use of that phrase, and glanced with sober furtiveness from him to Perse. In the grip of his wrath and worry, Arne had forgotten the sinister interpretation that usually accompanied such words.

To them Arne said, "Stuart's siding Forrest. If he sniffs back along my tracks—and he will—then we're all through. They won't be making much time with that buckboard." He scanned the faces of the two men. "You could catch up if you ride hard," he suggested.

Concho smiled. "Villapoco!" he whispered and waited for more.

Reese, a big roughneck twice Concho's size, shook his head humbly. "Forrest? After what he done to Temple? Not me, boss."

Arne's face grew red. "Forrest's only got one wing. Well, who winged him? You did. And what's Stuart? A damned old has-been. D'you let a worn-out rep scare *you*, Concho?"

"Me, no—nor any other kind of rep." The dapper little gunman continued smiling. "If I'm paid enough."

"Two thousand," Arne said. "Split it how you like."

"Cash on delivery?"

"*Pronto* on the barrel."

Concho turned to Reese. "Bill, we take it, eh? Is *muy mucho dinero*, and most generous."

"Now, look, I don't—"

"We take it," said Concho.

The great roiling thunderheads tore loose from the eastern hills, exposing a strip of stars, and raced westward with the moon.

"I wish," Stuart remarked, riding behind the buckboard, "we'd get rain. Sure need it. But we won't," he predicted from long knowledge of the country and its climate. "It'll drift right on over an' fall in Arizona. Or California. We oughta charge 'em freight."

Wade drove the buckboard team steadily on toward Maya, left-handed. His wounded right arm was too stiff to swing the whip, and his fears ate at him. Did Stuart actually believe he could get him to jail this night?

"Sheriff," he pleaded. "My gun. You can trust me. I won't make any break, I swear it to you. If—"

"No," Stuart said. "You're a prisoner because it's best for all concerned. I never gave any prisoner any gun and I don't mean to start now."

"But they'll—"

"Leave it be," Stuart snapped. "I do my own shootin'."

They traveled unhurriedly, Stuart making talk once in a while, Wade taciturn, to Bend, where the crowding prevalence of grayish-white tufa rock directed the old Miles Trail to angle a double S before straightening out again.

There in the high-sided cut, Stuart announced quietly, "This'll do. Pull in an' wait. Somebody's trailin' us." He reined his horse around and walked it back some distance.

The hush allowed hoofbeats to be heard. Wade stepped down into the road, carried the lines to a *piñon* stump, and tied the team. Then he walked slowly back to the first narrow curve. He wished to God he had his gun.

Of course, Stuart was only doing this to stop a range war, and Louise probably would be safe enough with Beth Tarey. He could just string along . . . he could, that is, if he wasn't so sure Stuart had long passed his peak.

Too long past his peak to handle this. He wished he had that g——

"All right, that's far enough!" Stuart's hail was a wispy sound against the hoofbeats. "Pull up there!"

The riders were coming head-on. A shot lashed the night, and after that a confusion of gunfire. Somebody's heels drummed the ribs of a horse. Brush and dwarfed *piñon* crashed to the passage of that one, charging off the road. Wade ran forward.

Stuart lay face-down on the road. His horse was gone. In his right hand he held his snub-nosed pocket pistol; in his left, Wade's heavy sixgun. A horseman was smashing around in the brush, cursing loudly. Another fought his plunging horse farther on down the road, voiceless in a contest for mastery.

Wade tore his gun from Stuart's hand and speared two shots into the boiling tangle ahead. Somebody cried out briefly. A riderless horse plunged past, empty stirrups swinging wildly, and the man in the brush yelled, "Bill, how you doin'?"

"Not so good!" Wade called. He whipped the brush with his shots. Another horse, frantic, rushed into the road, planted all four feet in an uncertain slide, and whistled its terror of a world gone mad.

It was Stuart's horse. Wade jumped and caught the free reins. He hauled aboard, necked it around, and put it to the brush. Having recognized Concho's voice, he shouted, "I'm coming after you, Concho!" There was a distant, fading pounding and crashing, a draining away of a voice cursing in English and Spanish. In the cloud-blackened obscurity Wade cursed back, reloaded his gun from the shell-loops in his belt, and fought the horse onto the road.

He tied the horse and went to Stuart, who was rolling his head. "How bad are you hurt?"

Stuart tried to sit up. He said, "Dammit to hell, when a coupla two-bit toughs can beat me, it's time to quit. Dammit to hell, I must be getting old." A bloody wound, black in the cloudy darkness, covered one side of his head. "Kindly get me to town, will you?"

Wade left him and paced down the road to a motionless object spread out on the hard-beaten ground. He knelt beside it and said, "Fluke shot. I fired wild."

Bill Reese muttered, "I know. Makes us even. Luck o' the game. Hell." He seemed to ponder on the hell of it. The breath sucked in noisily and blew out his bullet-torn lungs. "It's tough. I wish—"

He didn't go on and say what it was that he wished.

"Sorry," Wade said. "It was you or me, both times."

"Man, I don't hold it against you. How could I, what I done? My time's run out, that's all." Reese pushed himself up and said strongly, "You better look out for her. Bassett tol' Perse to finish her. That's a hell of a thing. A girl. Ain't it?"

Wade put an arm around him and supported him. "Yeah. You mean Bassett let Perse take her out of Los Portales?"

"Let him? Hell, he told him." Bill Reese rested against Wade's arm. "That bastard."

"Where?" Wade asked. "Where'd Perse take her?"

Reese breathed, "I wish—"

His voice broke into fragments of whispery sound without sense, and ceased altogether when his head rolled back. "Sorry," Wade said again, and meant it. He was not hardened to this yet. Bill Reese was one of the Gunsight men with whom he could easily have struck up a friendship under other circumstances. A tough hand, like the rest, but no more so than any cowpuncher became, riding for a tough outfit on the make. Arne Bassett's influence had strongly marked all of them, bringing out the worst in them.

Wade drew the dead man off the trail, and stood looking down, somber eyed. His hand fished in his pocket for tobacco and papers, but he brought it out empty, reluctant to strike a match. At that moment the clouds at last won their race with the moon; the pale light rushed over the trail and showed pitilessly the broken features of the dead man. Wade swung away. The passing time prodded him and he hurried in a limping sprint to Stuart's horse.

Stuart had got to his feet. Evidently abandoning any thought of going it horseback, he was slowly pacing up Bend to the buckboard with all the strained, dogged care of a drunken man trying to act sober. Wade called after him, "You'll have to get to town by yourself—I'm taking off after Perse!"

CHAPTER 18

I T WAS a good strong team that Perse drove. The buggy seemed to swish through the moonlit night, promptly responsive to a crack of the whip, giving him a sense of power. In quick gulps he had taken on more than half a pint of Beth's whiskey. It glowed him now and he felt no pain. It did not mellow him; drink always accentuated his dislikes.

Occasionally he slid a glance at Louise, seated on his left side and sunk in some kind of fear-ridden coma. She wasn't giving any trouble.

By God, she better not! Whacked him on his head with a poker and made a fool of him. Her, this white-faced little bit. Damn her!

He figured he knew what was required of him. Arne had put it in plain enough words: *Take care of her right.* Okay. Arne knew what he was doing. Pretty soon Arne would be the big man of Principe, the kingpin. And he, Colin Perse, the kid from Poverty Street, would be ramrod of the great T Anchor. Folks would go out of their way to oblige him, like they did now for Deac Shanter.

That was a picture. All that stood in the way was this white-faced bit. Hell. In that getaway from the bank robbery at Rostero he'd knocked a woman down and ridden his horse over her. It had bothered him some, but not for long. This wouldn't bother him long, either, if he did it right.

Black Walls came up, impassively forbidding; twenty miles of centuries-old anguished lava that somehow he felt akin to. It rose in the desert like a million fingers splayed against the encroachment of mere man.

Louise shuddered suddenly and made a muffled cry at the sight of it.

The sound rasped across Perse's nerves; it shook him and caused him to raise the whip at her. She cringed. He was afraid she would jump from the buggy, so he lowered the whip and growled, "It's all right." A straining impatience tugged at him and fired a kind of brightness in his milky blue eyes. He hit the team, and the buggy bowled at a spanking gait through the cut into the silent yard of Circle 7.

Louise cried out again, involuntarily, from fearful memory of this place. The distraught wildness of her cry warned Perse. His hands were fully occupied with the lines and whip. For all his venom, he had the usual male horror of a woman in hysterics.

"All right, all right," he grumbled. He reined the team hard around and shot out of the yard. "I'll take you to a better place."

Out of the cut, he swung west along the ragged great face of Black Walls. His intended destination was a long-abandoned old sheep camp midway between Circle 7 and the stage road, but his patience refused to hold out that far. Within a short half-mile he hauled the team to halt and said to Louise, not looking at her, "Here we are. Get down."

He ground-reined the team, doing everything with meticulous care and taking up unnecessary time; for a reluctance had now come upon him and he shied off from what he had to do. Riding that woman down, at Rostero, had been an entirely unpremeditated and necessary act. This had to be done in cold blood.

He shivered as he pointed the way to Louise. Where he had pulled in, there was a break in the regiment of giant lava. The relieving thought came to him: *Lose her in the Walls!*

That was all he had to do. Men had gone missing in the mammoth maze of Black Walls and not even their

buzzard-picked bones had been found. In the sheer per-
pendicular madness of Black Walls, horizontal points of
compass lost all meaning. You had to know the stars,
what could be seen of them within the cramping frame
of towering lava outcrops. He had ridden open range and
rough country most of his life. With his trained sense of
direction, plus a clear patch of sky, he could not get lost
anywhere.

"Walk on," he told Louise. "Right through there." In
his tight impatience to get this thing done and get away,
he shoved her on ahead, making her hurry, giving her
no chance to note where she was going.

The empty night gave out a murmur of sound: the
rhythmic beat of a hard-running horse. It infuriated him.
Why, now of all times, did somebody have to come down
to this God-forsaken place? He pushed and steered the
stumbling girl faster on down the winding passages, deeper
and deeper into Black Walls. By some trick of acoustics
the hoofbeats grew briefly loud, then faded all of a sudden
and died out. The unknown rider, he figured, must have
turned off east somewhere. Tremendously relieved, he
wiped a hand over his itching face, smearing the sweat-
loosened dried blood. His gashed head began throbbing
unbearably. He glared at the girl before him, and was able
without much effort to work up a malevolent spite that
demanded release in action.

"Wait a minute," he commanded. This was plenty far
enough. She'd never find her way out. Even for him it
wasn't going to be simple. "I—I got to go back to the
buggy for something. You wait here."

The silent black horror of the place was having its impact on her; she must have received some perception of
his intent to desert her. She wailed, "No, no!" and ran
after him.

It rasped the last thread of his nervous temper. A hard
breath gusted out of him, ending on a tinny high-voiced,
"Gahdamn!" He whirled around and struck out blindly
at her. His fist caught her on the forehead and knocked
her down. Then he ran away.

It was not within the limit of possibilities that he should
retrace with any exactness that tortuous course, and he
didn't try. The best he could do was to fix north and keep
working in that direction. The prevailing slant of the

crevices and passages was roughly east-west. It meant scrambling half a mile back and forth, and perhaps progressing north no more than fifty yards. Two or three times he thought he was being followed. A feverish desire to get away, akin to panic, drove him on and would not let him halt to investigate.

When he reached the break and saw the waiting buggy in the moonlight, he blew a sighing oath of relief. Fearing to startle the high-spirited team, he made himself slow down and walk forward. The horses shot their ears at him suspiciously, and he talked to them as he came up. Sensing at once his dark mood, they crowded uneasily away from him. He freed the lines and seated himself in the buggy.

In the act of starting off, he caught a repeated sound like breathless sobbing, and he threw a look up and around, incredulous. The small figure that came running into the break, holding its heavy skirt to keep from tripping on the hem, cried a sob-shattered word to him.

He snatched his carbine and reared up in the buggy. His bulging outraged glare clung to the running girl. He yelled madly and fired.

The team shied and slung the buggy hard onto the off-wheels. He was pitched out headlong, as if a carpet had been jerked from under his feet. It came so quickly that he had no time to use the cat-like ability of a cowpuncher to choose the manner of his fall. The back of his left shoulder hit the ground while his legs still flailed the air, and he felt something tear loose.

He rolled over, after a minute, and elbowed himself up onto his knees, too hurt to curse. He swayed there and was sick. The sounds of the runaway team and jolting buggy leveled off to one steady sound. Behind him in the break was only the dead silence of Black Walls. He could have imagined the sobbing, running little figure. It might be lying there or it might not, and he positively was not going to look.

Some long-forgotten scruple rose to warn him that he had committed a terrible and unforgivable deed tonight. He hid his mind from it, got miserably to his feet and lurched on the trail of the buggy. Torn tendons knifed agony into his left shoulder. He hoped the team would halt instead of drifting all the way back to Los Portales, and that he wouldn't meet anybody. From habit he touched his holster and felt his gun still in it. His guilt would not let him think of the carbine.

CHAPTER 19

Wade had been sure Perse would head for Circle 7. The Black Walls hideout offered so many advantages over Gunsight that he'd come here at a pelting gallop, intent on coming to grips with the mottle-faced ramrod before Perse had a chance to hole up securely.

But now, backing out of Circle 7 after a vain search, he was torn by anxiety, afraid that he had guessed amiss. Perse must have taken Louise to Gunsight after all. He had wasted time coming here. He would be way too late to prevent Perse from doing what Bill Reese swore Bassett had ordered him to do. Maybe he ought to . . .

Then a single shot echoed against the front barrier of Black Walls and across the blighted range like a boom of a cannon. He heeled his borrowed horse out of Circle 7 and when he cleared through the cut he sighted a rig racing northward up the range. He took out after it on a dead run.

That rig was rolling, apparently choosing the worst possible ground. It bounced and swayed crazily, but not until he beat within fair seeing distance in the moonlight did Wade realize that it lacked a driver. He swarmed in on the near side, mistrusting his right arm, and pounded abreast. He reached far down for a trailing line with his left hand. The bolting team dodged, nearly overturning the buggy.

On his second try he caught the cheek-strap of the near horse. He hung on, checking the speed of his mount and forcing over, until the team had to run a wide half-circle and slack down. He wrestled the pair to a standstill, slid off his horse and took stock of what he'd captured.

He gathered up the stamped lines, tested them, found them still serviceable. Holding to them warily, he tied Stuart's saddlehorse behind the buggy, took the driver's seat and drove back toward Black Hills.

The combination of team, buggy and trailing horse raised a racket. He could make out only a shadowed hint of tracks lining backward in the moonlight, and he thought in cruel despair, "It's already done. I'm too late. That shot killed her."

He drove directly along those barely visible tracks. A paler hue broke across the foreground where the blighted grass ceased altogether to exist and left exposed the silvery yellow sand. A small shadow, as of an animal, scuttled backward over that pale streak, hurrying to Black Walls. It paused and settled, foreshortened. . . .

The flash of the shot seemed ten feet long. The snarled reverberations of its solid crash seemed to roll like slow thunder above the earth. Something whistled *phut!* past him and sang its dry rattle of forcibly displaced air far behind.

He drew his gun with his left hand and loosed a shot in return. But the animal shadow was scuttling off again. The team spooked, reared, while Stuart's stolid horse gave out puffs of annoyed disgust. Wade took the whip to the team and ran them on. The shifting shadow melted into the deep covering of Black Walls, like a wolf backing into its lair.

There was a break in the upthrust of lava. Wade pulled the team in. Tying them steady posed a problem, for nothing grew here. He solved it by hobbling their forefeet with the lines, which cost time. Going forward then into the break, he kicked a solid object. Reaching down and feeling it, he found it to be a short rifle. He left it and went on.

From the back of the break a gun blared. He triggered twice at the spear of flame, then dropped and listened. The animal gasped and scrambled off somewhere.

Wade crept on after that rapidly retreating scurry. What he thought was a rock, lying to the left of his course, took on a softer and more recognizable outline on second look. He veered over to it quickly. His hand touched the cloth of Louise's dress.

He knelt, cursing whisperingly in a wild abandon to rage and grief and defeat. Passion burst, and he shouted, "Damn your rotten soul to everlasting hell, I'll get you for this!" It was not only Perse that his oath condemned.

Arne Bassett stood foremost. He was the man who had ordered this to be done.

But now he had to work fast. He slid his hands under Louise, picked her up, and carried her out of the break to the less shadow-veiled ground beside the buggy. She was small and very light. When he laid her down by the buggy, his right hand came away wet and sticky from her right side. But she moaned; she was alive.

Kneeling beside her, he made use of the trick of breathing deeply and informing himself that he positively could master this bad situation—a trick learned from other bad situations and close scrapes in his life. He worked out his five-inch jackknife, bared the blade, and with cool presumption cut the dress from the neck down to the waist. Then he cut open the fine linen camisole.

Louise's body gleamed white as bone in the moonlight, from neck to waist. There it blotched blackly. She was shot through the ribs, and bleeding from the back where the bullet had come out. A ragged hole, that. A blunt-nosed .44 from that sawed-off cylinder saddle-gun Perse carried.

Lacking bandages, Wade pressed his hand against the hole. He swore in despair. Louise moaned again. Frantically, he tugged out the camisole. It came in fuller volume than he hoped. He made strips of it, but they weren't long enough. Remembering her petticoats, he threw back her heavy skirt and went to work on them.

He made pads of the torn camisole, tied them into place with long strips of petticoat. And all the time he watched the break for Perse to come out, keeping his gun ready in his trousers' waistband. The bleeding was stopped, he guessed. He could do no more now for this forlorn little girl but get her to a doctor. He pulled the dress over her and picked her up very carefully.

She moaned again.

He said to her, "It's all right. I'll take care of you, honey." A powerful pity gentled his voice. "I've got you."

He laid her on the back seat of the buggy, still talking to her. He lifted his long legs over into the driver's seat in front, slapped the team, and headed north. Stuart's good horse tracked along behind, placidly ignorant of Wade's worry.

Hours ago, Arne Bassett must have learned from Concho of the fight at Bend. Not knowing of Bill Reese's dying disclosure, Arne had no reason to suspect Wade of riding south to Circle 7, but he and his Gunsight hands would certainly be out on the hunt for him by now. There was strong risk of running into some of them in Maya, or even before reaching it. Yet he could see no way of avoiding that risk. Louise was in urgent need of a doctor's care, and Doc Meek was in Maya.

He crossed the Calaveras ford at a slow walk, concerned with keeping the buggy from jolting too roughly on the stony bed. On the smooth-beaten stage road the team settled down to a fast, even pace requiring little encouragement.

The fair road afforded Wade opportunity to turn and assure himself that Louise was not rolling off the back seat. She seemed partly conscious now to some degree, for when her left arm slipped off the seat she made an effort to lift it. He twisted around, reached over, and put her arm back. Her fingers moved, closing on his as if wanting to hold onto them for comfort. He held her hand for an instant before having to turn his attention to the team and the road.

A horseman bobbed on the moonlit ribbon of Miles, coming down darkly, his easy-rocking lope sending forth a tattoo that spelled out deliberate purpose.

Wade tightened up on the lines. He could see that rider, therefore that rider could see him. There was no cover, no hiding, no place for a brush fight here. The empty land imposed an unescapable law: *You must meet him.*

He drew his gun and held it between his knees, keeping the team running. All he could do was meet the man, have it out with him. "And hope to Christ," he murmured, without intent of blasphemy, thinking of Louise.

"*Que es?*" he sang out, using the Mexican query in a hope to confuse and throw the man off, as the buggy and the rider shrank the intervening distance to pistol range. Before the reply came, he knew the man: the severe black coat, straight posture, unmistakable slant of the broad-brimmed hat.

Deac Shanter called forward, "Forrest? Pull in!" He circled his horse alongside in a slither of dust. His frigidly calm eyes took in everything while he reined his horse down.

"That the girl? She hurt?"

"Perse shot her."

"Uh. Follow me. We'll take her to Glory Spring."

"I'm taking her to Maya. To Doc."

"No you're not," Deac Shanter said. "You'd never get to Maya alive. Stuart's got more friends than he knows. Half the country's out after you for slamming a sneak shot at him while he was taking you in."

"I didn't gun Stuart. He can tell you."

"We'll talk that over at Glory Spring," said Deac. "We pull off west 'bout a mile up. We strike the trail two miles on." He paused. "How's Perse?"

"Somewhere in Black Walls. I think I hurt him."

"*Bueno*," Deac responded coldly. He didn't say another word until they reached the working headquarters of T Anchor.

When Wade and Deac came out from Deac's own room, where Deac had helped place Louise in his own bed, they left a light on and the door ajar. In the big main room Deac commented, "Couple ribs nicked. Maybe not bad. No bits of bone where the bullet came out." Then he added reflectively, "She's had a pretty tough time of it. Should have a good man to take care of her."

"She's got to have a doctor," Wade said.

Deac nodded impersonally and strolled on out to the mudcaked gallery. Wade heard him call a name. A voice answered promptly from the bunkhouse and somebody came running.

To the man he had called, Deac said, "Get Doc Meek here, Charlie, if Stuart's not too bad off. Tell Doc we got a hurt girl here. Anybody else, tell 'em we got a man with a broken leg. Put a fresh team to that buggy, an' take it. That's all, Charlie."

Deac came back in and stared at Wade. "Look, you. They say you gunned Stuart, just as Concho and Reese caught up, wanting to make sure Stuart got you to jail. You shot old Stuart. You killed Reese. You took Stuart's horse and made your getaway. So they all say, and they're all after you."

"Why didn't they find me before now?"

"Concho took a spill in the dark, getting away from you. I was at Beth's when he walked in and told his story.

He'd lost his horse. I set out for Bend. Found Hugh Stuart lying by that buckboard. Took him into Maya and got Doc Meek. Took both of them to Catherine Larmor's house." Deac shrugged his broad, well-clad shoulders. "Time we got him worked on, Concho was in town putting out his story. Bassett was rounding up a posse—he called it that—to hunt you down for killing Reese and damn near blowing Stuart's head off. He sent word to the Starvations crowd to come in. I guess there's about two hundred men kicking up the landscape for you in every known direction."

Wade asked, "Were you looking for me when you rode south down Miles, or for Perse?"

"Perse," Deac said. He got a full bottle and two glasses from the Spanish-style *trastero*-fronted cupboard, and set them on the table. "In all the commotion in Maya, I happened to recall some mention of Perse and Louise. Thought I'd look into it. Of course, Perse would naturally take the girl back to Circle 7." He pinned a pale look on Wade. "How did *you* know?"

Wade gave his story of the fight at Bend. "Those two were out to get Stuart and me. Stuart wanted to fish to the bottom. He as good as told Bassett so. Said he'd get off a message to Villapoco, where Bassett married Louise. He'd sorta swung over to my side after he saw Louise."

Deac filled both glasses, emptied his in one gulp, looked at it and said, "Here's how you stand. Half the country is after you. Stuart's hurt bad and can't talk. What witnesses have you got left for your story? Luttrell's dead. Perse, he's Bassett's man all the way. What's on your mind next?"

Wade said stonily, "I came down here to find Louise and take here back home. I've found her."

Deac shook his head. "Try a run for it? You won't get out of the Principe alive. Nor her, if you're right about Bassett—and like Hugh Stuart, I'm thinking you are. No, Forrest. You got to get Bassett first. Once you get him—"

"I think," Wade interrupted, "you put the fix on Frank Brouk. He was getting too close to Beth." He stared at Deac over the table and said, "Now it's Bassett. I've always looked on you as a big man. Is Arne Bassett so big you're scared to take him on?"

Deac did not rear up and show anger. He lit a cigar and puffed out the match. "Arne and Beth are about engaged to marry. Beth owns T Anchor. Me, I'm T Anchor's ramrod. Where would gunning down Arne put me?"

"I'd call myself smart if I could operate like you," Wade said meditatively. "I grant that you can't stay ramrod by shooting every man Beth might think of marrying. But if they knock off each other, you're in. As her husband, eh, Deac?"

The faintest of sardonic smiles flitted across Deac Shanter's wide, strong mouth. Then suddenly, startlingly the inhuman calmness broke. His muscled brows bunched, scowling, and fire glowed in his deep set gray eyes. "A man can't help it—the woman he wants—what kind of woman she is. I've wanted Beth a long time. Since I saw her picture, before I met her. I made up my mind then I'd marry her. Why the hell else would I have taken on this T Anchor, and given old Simon Tarey my sworn oath I'd hold it together as long as I lived? You think I'd scheme and work for—" he almost shouted the word— "*pay?* If it wasn't for her, T Anchor could go to hell for my part!"

Wade nodded. He knew many times Deac Shanter must have secretly rebelled like a caged hawk against the confining bars erected by his sworn oath; for he had always been masterless, a free-roving gambler and gunfighter, a lone wolf who had garnered a blazing reputation in tough places where life ran to a rapid tempo and to miss a step meant disaster.

"Get Arne Bassett," Deac said.

"If I do, what then?"

"I pay my debts. I'll see you and that girl safe out of the country, if it takes me and every T Anchor man I got to do it. That's my promise. Good enough for you?"

"And if I don't?"

"Then the hell with you."

Wade thought of the hurt little girl in the quiet room, of Bassett's command to Perse, of his own grim promise back in Black Walls. He had almost forgotten that last. "All right," he said in an intolerably weary, hope-robbed sigh. "I guess Bassett and I would have to shoot it out, anyhow, somewhere."

Deac refilled the glasses. "It seems so," he allowed, falling back to his normal dry tone. He rose and went out and called over to the bunkhouse, "Victoriano! Go get your daughter—the eldest one, Rosina—and ask her to come here, *por favor*, to attend the lady."

"*Sí!* Right 'way!"

Wade let his head sink, closed his eyes, and slept.

Toward morning the buggy returned from Maya. Doc Meek came into the house with Catherine Larmor. They looked thoroughly tired, having been up most of the night with Sheriff Hugh Stuart. Doc Meek, a large, stout man, looked wishfully at the bottle on the table. He was a heavy drinker, so of course it was said of him that he was a drunken genius: a better doctor, drunk, than any other in the world, sober.

Deac Shanter asked about Stuart while showing them to the room where Louise lay. Doc replied flippantly, "Couldn't kill the old cuss with canister and an axe," and he and Catherine went into the bedroom and Catherine closed the door.

They were in there for what seemed a long time. Once, Louise cried out, afterward murmuring for a minute or two.

Catherine came out first. Wade asked, "How is she?"

"She'll be all right," Catherine answered dully. She didn't meet his eyes. She sank tiredly into a chair and rested her head back. "Won't she, Doc?"

Doc said, "Oh, yes. Bad shock, but not too much damage. Terribly nervous, poor girl. Says Bassett's foreman tried to murder her. I won't let that go any farther. Thought I should tell you, Deac. You're footing my bill." He snuffled a laugh.

Reverting to seriousness, he said, "She wants to see you, Forrest."

Wade went in to Louise. The room gave an impression of largeness because it was barely furnished. It contained nothing that could not claim direct utility. The bed, too, seemed large, Louise being so small in it. She murmured gratefully, "Wade Forrest," and moved to free her arms from under the bedclothes. That she was unable to do.

Pain wrenched her pale little face. Then with a rare courage she smiled and uncovered her right hand. Wade took it in his and sat on the edge of the bed, saying, "Feeling better now?" A compassionate tenderness that was very familiar to him, and uncontrollable, made him say further, gently, "You're going to be all right, honey." Those were the words he had spoken so many times to Anna in her attacks of illness and black depression.

He had not thought to close the door, and to do so now would give rise to undue attention. Although weak, Louise's voice was softly clear. "Thank you, Wade, for taking care of me. Oh, thank you, thank you, thank you—"

A hush hung in the big main room, until Doc Meek cleared his throat noisily and banged an emptied glass on the table and proclaimed, "Rule of the country. Host pours the first one, then you serve yourself. Right, Deac?"

"Right," replied Deac soberly. "There's the bottle."

"Gentleman and a scholar!"

The bottle clinked. There was no other sound.

Louise's eyes lost focus, dimmed, closed. She fell asleep, her hand in Wade's. After a while Wade rose, tucked her hand back under the covers, and came quietly out. He asked Deac, "Is Stuart's horse ready?"

Deac's nod was slow and thoughtful.

Catherine raised her head. "Must you go?"

At the door he murmured, "Yes." It was not yet light outside, and he added absently, "G'night." He paced stolidly to the waiting horse, legged aboard the saddle and rode off.

CHAPTER 20

AROUND MIDMORNING Arne Bassett and four men of his crew morosely kicked their drooping horses up the bad trail to High Folds and trooped finally into the treeless draw of Gunsight headquarters.

Even Concho, by nature a cheerful and talkative little hoodlum, lacked the spirit to dig up a wryly bright quip. He had taken a terrific tongue-lashing from Arne, for his and Bill Reese's failure at Bend, and he still smarted from it. Arne said curtly to him now, "Tell Jose to fix us something to eat, quick, while we put up the horses." Concho nodded and rode on to the combination bunkhouse and kitchen.

The three other men didn't offer a word, not wanting to invite the lash of Arne's fierce temper. Arne Bassett was in a murderous mood. He had figured it out that Wade Forrest would certainly flee north after the fight at Bend and his escape from arrest. Where else? North was where Forrest had come from, and a man naturally headed for home when trouble lit a fire under him. North, sure, to Villapoco; to acquire there the evidence of that mad marriage. The man would not give up, but he wasn't a fool. His last and only bet was Villapoco. He would take off up into the Freyes and work north. That was his sensible course. He would leave tracks that could be followed, even in moonlight, by an expert tracker like Concho.

But there had been no tracks. Bassett and his force rode all the way to the steep foothills of Los Freyes, and spent all night searching north and south. Forrest had cut off in some other direction. Where? For God's sake, where?

Bassett and the three men dismounted stiffly and off-saddled. They watered the horses, fed them a little grain and turned them into the alfalfa corral. They trudged up to the bunkhouse. At the door, Concho met Bassett with a solemn look, poked a thumb at a bunk, and walked off down to the kitchen end.

Perse lay on that bunk. His feet stuck out, unbooted, two clotted lumps of burst blisters and blood and glued shreds of socks. Dried blood filled the socket of his right eye. He looked horrible.

Staring down at him, Arne Bassett demanded, "What the hell are you doing here? Where's Louise?"

"His shot chipped rock in my eye," Perse complained. "The girl? I done what you said. I took care of her right, this time." He heaved a breath. "She's—dead. Only thing is, he came along. He took her off, her an' the buggy. I walked here."

Arne Bassett threw up his arms. "You fool! I didn't tell you to kill her! God Almighty, that's—that's—you've murdered a girl!"

His brain meshed to work. He lowered his arms, thinking fast and craftily. "He took her to Maya, then," he said. "He'll cave up till Stuart's in shape to talk. Then he'll do *his* talking. Sure." Already he was considering how to bend this calamity to his advantage, squandering no regret on the girl he had married. To him, pity was at best a pose; he never for an instant believed in its sincerity. It was just something you were expected to show on occasion, like pulling a long face at a funeral while privately damning the waste of time.

To Perse he said, "You've got to get out o' here. This is one bobble too many you've pulled. I won't take the risk of siding a man who's murdered a girl. Not in these parts. I'll give you a horse and some money. You hit for Old Mexico."

"God! Arne, I can't," Perse groaned. "I'm done up. Look at me. Have a heart, man. Let me—"

Bassett grasped his blood-stained shirt and hauled him roughly out of the bunk onto the floor, where Perse tumbled awkwardly to his knees, his thin-lipped mouth wide open and gasping.

"Get out, damn you!"

Over his shoulder Bassett snapped to the mute, staring men, "Saddle a horse for him. He's leaving."

They saddled the horses. They dragged him from his bunk and carried him out into the yard and hoisted him into the saddle. He wasn't as weak as all that, actually. He was just dazed and incredulous. He had stuck by Arne Bassett through thick and thin. Gunsight was the great hope and promise of his mean life, offering him the vision of personal importance, prestige. He had given everything he could to it: hard work, dishonesty, dangerous activity in the night, even loyalty and a faithful regard for Arne's welfare.

With slow comprehension of his plight came fear. He was hurt and alone. He had murdered a girl and when that was known every man would hunt him. There wasn't a chance to make it to Mexico. He had no friends to turn to.

"God," he moaned. "I gotta get out o' this jackpot. I gotta do somethin'. . . ."

But they ignored him. He had barely cleared the Gunsight yard before Arne told Concho, "You and Segura and Kentuck saddle fresh horses. One for me, too. We're going to Maya. I think Forrest's there. And Stuart. You

got another chance to win some money, Concho. Don't
fall on your face again. Sabe?"

"*Sí*," said Concho. "We'll get 'em. Where?"

"Catherine Larmor's house. That's most likely." Arne
squinched his eyes in thought. "Look. Forrest killed Reese.
Forrest killed Louise. Now Forrest kills Stuart. You saw
it all. Two thousand dollars?"

"*Sí!*" said Concho.

CHAPTER 21

IN THE RISING DAWN, Wade had worked circuitously
into Maya by way of straggling West Street. He put up
Stuart's horse in the little stable behind the Sheriff's office,
and from there he skirted on foot north around the silent
town, crossed Miles, and bent south behind the buildings
on the east side.

Toland's was his objective. He had in mind the possibility of slipping unseen up the back stairs of the hotel
and getting onto the flat roof. As with most buildings in
this land of Pueblo Indian and old Spanish influence, the
roof had a raised fire-wall running around it, with slotted
canales to drain off rain. This would afford him a vantage
from which to observe the town.

Bassett was bound to come in some time during the day.
After that he'd have to plan according to the chances
events and fate afforded him. Until then, all he could do
was remain unseen until the final opportunity came to face
Bassett.

But luck wasn't with him right now.

The rear door of Harrison's Emporium gaped wide
open and a lamp burned inside. Wade paused and swore
silently: he had to pass that door. Whoever was inside had
certainly heard him, and would get inquisitive if he turned
back. He walked on, holding his head away and scratch-
ing his cheek with a masking hand.

"Good morning, Mr. Forrest," said Harrison politely.

Wade halted, made a half-turn, and stepped inside with

his left hand shoved down under his coat. "Good morning, Mr. Harrison. You get to work early."

It was Harrison's office, a cramped little space at the back of the store. The shaded lamp stood on a table that served as a desk. Seated facing the open door, Harrison laid his pen carefully alongside an open ledger. "Yes, sir. I'm usually here before daylight, to check the books and get things ready.

"You've got good eyes."

The storekeeper made no pretense of mistaking Wade's meaning. He looked steadily at Wade and murmured, "I sold you the clothes you're wearing, you know."

Wade uttered a short laugh. "So you did. I forgot. I wish you'd forget, too. You know, I guess, I can't afford to let anybody see me, don't you?"

Harrison steepled his fingers and rested his chin on them. When serving Wade ahead of his regular customers, that Saturday, he had revealed a streak of independent nonconformity. He showed it again, now. He was a rebel, dreaming under the layers of tradesman's manners.

"Mr. Forrest," he said, "no customer of mine has ever had occasion to take a gun to me." His eyes rested fleetingly on Wade's left hand. "I've been in business a long time. My best customers have been, ah, men in violent disagreement with the law. Straight cash and no haggling, you know. And I've been glad to oblige them with little extra courtesies which were always fully appreciated."

He shut his eyes. "Sorry, I'm very sleepy," he yawned. "The door there on the left leads upstairs to the store room. Nobody goes there but me."

At that door, Wade looked back at him. Harrison kept his eyes shut, apparently slumbering over the ledger, seeing and hearing nothing. Because of some truant quirk, this colorless, servile-mannered storekeeper drew mischievous relish from his hobby of aiding men who were out-of-law.

And, because of Harrison, Wade was watching from the corner window of the store room when the T Anchor buggy bowled into town. Deac Shanter was driving, with Catherine and Doc Meek in the back seat. The buggy turned up East Street, taking Catherine home. Presently it appeared again. Deac dropped off Doc Meek at his office-and-home on the east side of the main street, then wheeled smartly over to the west side, fetching up at Wright's. He halted in front of the livery and called through the open door, and Wright's stableman came out to water the team.

Next, Deac walked back across the street to Toland's. He spoke to a group of men on the boardwalk's edge and they heaved up from their loafing to follow him into the barroom. They were showing signs of excitement. Other men along the street, seeing the commotion, moved hurriedly on to Toland's to learn what it was that Deac Shanter had to say.

Wade wondered, himself. But he had to sweat and wait.

Later, four riders dusted abreast into town, from the south. Before they struck the main street, Wade recognized the straight, compactly built figure of Arne Bassett; the small and rakishly dapper Concho; then Segura and the man who went only by the name of Kentuck—a long, thin, sick man whose expression permanently registered a saturnine discontent.

At that moment the main street was empty. From the corner window of Harrison's store room, Wade watched Bassett fix an immediate stare on the T Anchor buggy standing before Wright's livery. Bassett threw up an imperious hand and all four riders reined in. They made a curiously impressive tableau, the four men leaning forward, reins drawn hard on stiff-halted horses, their eyes concentrated in one direction. The most casual glance could read purpose in these men, implacable purpose. No gang of wild-bunch outlaws, determined on raid and robbery, could have showed their intent more clearly.

It was curious, too, to observe the shortcomings of Bassett's mind. The man had intelligence. A moment of cool reflection could have told him that Wade—a hunted fugitive, a man on the dodge—would never have left the buggy there to mark his last stop. But Bassett was charged full of hot temper. He was out for blood and the buggy made it positive for him that the man he had to kill lay hiding here in Maya. He swung his feral stare at East Street, and neck-reined his horse slantwise across the street.

Concho and the other two Gunsight hands rode with him. They dismounted and tied up to the rickety hitchrack fronting Josefita's closed saloon on bad West Block.

There Bassett spoke to them, jabbing his forefinger at each in turn, as insistent as a lawyer coaching witnesses, giving them their orders. Concho thumbed at East Street and made some sort of describing motion, and Bassett nodded.

Wade left the window and ran down the stairs from the storeroom. Harrison, alone in the store, must have heard him, but didn't look up from fluffing out a yard of colored dress-goods for display. Going out the rear door, Wade sprinted the half-block to the back of Catherine Larmor's boarding house and opened the kitchen door without knocking.

Catherine was helping Katey at the kitchen table—getting ready that eternally recurrent midday meal, of course. A lost night's sleep could not be made up the next day when you ran a boarding house for a living. The men had to be fed. Catherine had been up all night taking care of Stuart. Then she had ridden down to Glory Spring with Doc Meek to help care for Louise, and come back home again. By reasonable reckoning she should have been limply played out. Yet here she was, still on her feet and hard at work, her firm young body as erect as ever; a gallant girl, clean and strong and guarding within herself a full force of feminine vitality.

The fair head and the dark one came around, at the sound of the opened door, with that half impatient yet warm interest of women busy with everyday chores. The work stopped. Katey scanned Wade's face and wiped her hands decisively on her apron, evidently sensing that the work would not go on. Catherine asked, "Wade?" in a voice containing one dominant query.

Pushing the door shut behind him, Wade stepped on into the dining room and through it to the hallway, where he stood listening intently. Catherine and Katey came up behind him.

He said, "Arne Bassett's on his way here, with Concho and two more. They'll demand to search for me." He paused. "I—I even think Bassett would finish off Stuart if he got the chance. That's why I came. They're not pushing in here if I can stop them."

Catherine whisked past him, slid the bolt on the front door, and returned. She would have spoken, but he spread a hand for silence. In a continuation of that gesture he drew his gun and stuck it in his belt on the right side, its butt to the front.

Somebody, trying to be quiet, could be heard softly crunching gravel alongside the house to the rear. Between the house and the neighboring one ran a carriage drive, relic of more prosperous days when Catherine's parents lived. The prowler had made the mistake of expecting the driveway to be hard-packed; it hadn't been used for years and winter's freezes had heaved and loosened it.

Katey slipped off, agile as a stripling for all her tremendous size, and returned to report, "Mike Segura. A tough Mex, that one. He's in the back yard. Behind the garbage cans, watching the kitchen door. Oh, man, dear!" She touched Wade on his back. "What's going to happen to you?" She began to cry.

Catherine said, "Katey Bloom, you hush up!" She stood beside Wade. "We'll handle this!"

Somebody twisted the knob of the front door. The bolt held the door fast. The inside knob twirled to its normal position. Then came a heavy and authoritative knock.

Wade murmured to Catherine, "Get back. That's Bassett." During the brief moment it took him to pace up the hall to the door, he cast a speculative search for Concho and Kentuck, and found it fruitless. They could be anywhere. On tap behind Bassett, or fifty yards off. One thing only was certain: this house was surrounded by four men inexorably determined to kill him and, more than likely, Stuart.

The bolt slipped easily from its socket, clicking a warning to the man outside. It could not be helped. Gathering all his senses up tight, Wade swung the door in and let go of it and plunged forward. He chested solidly into Bassett. The door crashed wide open and rebounded almost shut behind him.

Bassett's stance was that of a boxer prepared to slug, left foot and shoulder foremost to the door, right arm held back, slightly bent. The one deviation was his right fist, gripping the butt of the holstered gun strapped to his thigh. Wade's lunge and collision had stolen the couple of seconds he needed to recognize his enemy and upset his plan.

Jostled, Arne had to throw his left leg far back to maintain balance. This brought his broad body around so that

his right side was forward, his right hand fully exposed
on the gun-butt. Wade followed closely, pushing with his
chest, his hands hanging empty at his sides. Bassett would
never pull his gun, this close, unless he absolutely had to.
*Never pull your gun in reaching distance of the proposed
deceased*, enjoined the grimly humorous old maxim. Arne
gave way a half-step more, then got his legs braced and
shouldered Wade a battering-ram blow.

They stood straining silently against each other on the
white-painted gallery, their faces not six inches apart.
The hard handsomeness of Bassett's features had coarsened
subtly since Wade first saw the man. Bold temper had
become stark deviltry. The dark, fiery eyes flashed a bitter
courage beyond any mere recklessness, and the mouth too
was bitter. Like many men before him, Bassett had found
that crime was cumulative. A lie led straight to a bigger
lie, and murder preceded murder.

While a part of Wade's mind remotely observed and
made note, his attention whisked past Bassett's face to
register in one sweeping glance the details of East Street.
Then he spotted Concho and Kentuck. Concho stood between two houses directly across the way, gun drawn,
brows cocked in wonder as to what he might contribute
to this unforeseen situation; he couldn't risk a shot because Bassett was in the way. Kentuck was moving out
onto the street, a few houses down on this side, and he
too looked puzzled.

Bassett brought his elbow forward in a wicked jab
that broke Wade's crowding pressure on him. He drew
off swiftly. Wade didn't follow. Bassett edged backward
to the gallery stairs, watching Wade's left hand intently.
At Los Portales he had learned that Wade did not yet
trust his right arm. He backed down to the first step, the
second, the third, and so to earth.

Wade stood still on the gallery, his left hand clasping
his stomach where Bassett's elbow had punched him. In
the act of doing so his sleeve had brushed open his coat,
giving a glimpse of the empty holster. Bassett got that
glimpse.

Another man might have smiled, showed a grin, however sneering and prematurely triumphant, according to
his nature and prevailing mood.

Wade scraped a cross-draw to the gun in the belt under

the right side of his coat. The ordinary noises of the street continued for an infinitesimal fraction of a second. A woman screamed something inside a house, in the tone of a mother admonishing her children. Bassett's left foot rested on the bottom step of the gallery, the right firmly planted below it. His hand raised for a straight shot.

Wade's bullet caught him in that coldly confident stance, and Bassett's bullet ripped a splintered groove in the top step. Wade fired again and lifted his eyes to Concho across the street.

That second shot drove Bassett off the bottom step. He backed away a pace, and coughed, twisting his head as if to make a remark to Concho. His knees gave out and he dropped to them. The force of the fall broke him in the middle, letting him bow over until his head struck the ground. He collapsed to one side, knees drawn up, mumbling, thinking he was rapping commands to Concho.

Another gun from another quarter blared into the shattered respectableness of East Street. Concho paced sedately out on his toes from between the two houses, both hands up to his sleek hair as though to smooth it. It was a familiar gesture varied only in that he left his hat and gun lying in the dirt.

Also, after the hair-smoothing gesture, Concho tumbled onto the street and stopped moving.

That gun sounded off once more, and Wade saw who was using it.

Deac Shanter, a tall black figure in the noonday blaze of sunlight, came striding around the corner from Toland's, into the middle of the street. He lashed a third shot. Kentuck shouted, then nothing more was heard from him. Segura ran out from behind Catherine's house, threw a wildly shocked look around, and dodged back and vanished.

Deac came on along the street, walking unhurriedly in the manner of a man having nothing of any importance on his mind to raise a ripple against quiet meditation. It was well-known that he wore two guns under his long black coat. He had drawn only one of them, and now he sheathed the weapon unconcernedly.

Yet even he cracked his composure and leaped aside as a horse whirled in headlong from the main street behind him. He spun around, leaped again, and caught the horse's bridle. His quickness and strength were amazing. The running horse slithered half around on crouched haunches. It would have spilled, except that Deac heaved its head up, using his left hand. With his right hand he steadied its rider. He did it all in one positive flow of motion.

"Why so ungodly fast, lady?" he drawled. "Horse run away with you? I told you that sidesaddle's worthless on a bronc!"

Riding the only sidesaddle ever seen in the Principe, Beth Tarey righted herself from kissing the horse's neck and demanded, "Where's Arne?" When she straightened up it could be seen that she held in her right hand a pistol, a big .54 U. S. N. smoothbore that had belonged to her seafaring father; a short-gun fashioned to blow a man down at ten paces. Several T Anchor riders swarmed thunderously into the street after her. All were armed, stiff of face; they jolted to halt and sat peering alertly about through their furious welter of dust.

"Where's Arne?" Beth repeated, with something like the voice of an angrily determined man, speaking to Deac.

In his same drawl, Deac answered, "Look and be quiet, lady. Over there." Coming from him, the words did not express insolence, but rather a kindly counsel.

Beth's gaze searched out. As though dowered with a forecast, and hampered by reluctance to verify it, her gaze touched everything else before resting at last on the curled, ungainly shape in the dirt at the foot of the gallery steps of Catherine Larmor's house.

There emerged a momentary shade of sorrow, regret for a dead love. Beth then handed her heavy pistol down to Deac and asked, "You killed him?"

Deac passed the pistol on to the nearest T Anchor man, and said, "No, lady. He came in for trouble and got it. Shot it out with Forrest." He motioned sparely at Wade on the gallery of Catherine's house. "Forrest won."

Beth dug her horse forward to the gallery. To Wade she said, "Perse came to Los Portales this morning. He talked about Arne. About him and that girl. His wife? Is that true?"

Wade heard the squeak of horror opening behind him. Catherine, certainly. He said woodenly to Beth, "I tried to tell you. Sure. He married her."

"And killed her?"

"No. He gave Perse that job. Perse took her down to Black Walls and shot her. But she's not dead."

Deac motioned at Wade. "He smoked Perse off and brought the girl to Glory Spring. Bullet hole through her ribs. Done on T Anchor range, by God! How d'you like that, lady?" And to Wade: "I've got to be starting back. I'll give you a lift in the buggy." He followed Wade's long glance over the crowd gathering beyond the armed riders. "It's all right. Little while ago I broke the news it was Concho and Reese who jumped Stuart, so you're clear with the mob."

Beth Tarey spent no further regard on Arne. Knowledge of having been tricked, made a fool of, plainly struck a shattering blow at her self-confidence. Even the sustaining force of anger deserted her, for she threw an uncertain look around at all the staring faces and said to Deac hurriedly, "I'll—I'd like to ride out with you—"

"Surely, lady," Deac murmured. To the T Anchor men he said something about picking the trash up off the street before they left. "Come on, Forrest."

Wade turned to say a word or two to Catherine, but he was too late. She was closing the front door. He scanned it for a blank moment after the lock softly clicked.

Then Beth called to him, "Come on—Wade!"

Beth left her horse at Wright's and Deac ordered a fresh team. When the two-seated buggy was readied he waved briefly for Wade to climb into the rear, then as a matter of course started to hand Beth up front beside the driving seat. Beth, however, took a step aside and chose the back seat, leaving Deac with no more to do but sit alone and drive.

The rig cleared town and rolled down Miles. Sharing with Beth the rather close quarters of the seat, Wade wondered uncomfortably what Deac's thoughts were about it. Chiefly for the sake of breaking a silence that was growing awkward, he mused aloud, "Why would Perse turn against Arne Bassett?"

"From what he told me," Beth said indifferently, "I gather it was Arne who turned against him. Fired him. Perse was a sight. Half blind, crippled, sick, scared and mad. He asked to hide at Los Portales, but of course I couldn't have that. I gave him some money and sent one of the Mexicans along to see him out of the country."

Sitting up forward, driving, Deac remarked without looking around, "It'll be all right to drop you off at Los Portales, then."

"No," Beth answered. "I'll go on with you to Glory Spring and take care of that poor girl."

Deac said nothing. He swung the whip and hit both horses.

There came another long silence. The swaying of the rig brought Beth's shoulder to brushing Wade's occasionally. Wade next grew aware of her face bent toward him as though she had asked a question that he had not heard. He turned his head, and found her eyes full of that unspoken query. They held the gaze between them, until Beth leaned back with a satisfied little sigh. She was already engaged in rebuilding her feminine self-confidence.

CHAPTER 22

At Glory Spring headquarters Deac drew up at the house and sang out, "Ed!" To the man who came around the bunkhouse in response, he put a question.

"Did Victoriano bring his daughter to look after the young lady?"

"Sure did. She's in there now."

Deac nodded, handed the lines over to Ed, and while stepping down laid an inscrutable glance at Beth. Her full lips straightened perceptibly. Wade handed her out of the rig. On the ground, starting forward to the gallery steps, she paused and said straight before her, "I'm going in to see how things are." After that her eyes came around to Deac. "This *is* T Anchor, isn't it?" Deac made no reply, and she went on into the house.

Wade surprised a stain of deep sympathy in Deac's eyes. It washed out as Deac moved and spoke directly to him.

"I made a deal with you, Forrest."

"Just so," agreed Wade. He studied his left hand, not really seeing it. "Anyhow, the case is changed now. I don't anticipate any trouble getting Louise and myself out of the Principe, when she's well enough to travel."

"The case is changed," Deac agreed in turn. "Now I'll see you north to wherever it is you have to take her, and if there's anything wrong there I'll help you right it. I pay my debts."

"'Out of debt, out of danger,'" Wade quoted absently.

Some faint movement worked across Deac's lips, soon gone, leaving him as calmly impassive as ever. He reached into the breast pocket of his coat and brought out two cigars; after they fired up, the two men stood smoking for a long spell, saying no more. The gallery steps were immediately behind them, but neither man would relax and sit down. Beth, coming out at last onto the gallery, caused them to glance around up at her. Catching something in her manner and expression, Deac wheeled fully around. His eyes hung searchingly on her.

She slowly descended the steps to Wade, and laid a hand on his arm. "I have a—a message for you."

He nodded, waiting, crushing many thoughts from his mind in order to receive what she had to say. The solemnity of her tone then cut at his attention, and he winced. "You mean—she—Louise is—?"

"No, no!" A tinge of impatience lifted her tone. "Of course not. She's going to be all right. Got a good deal more sense now, too, than when I saw her last."

"Then what?"

"The message is from her."

"Yes?"

"She asked me to tell you."

"Well?"

"Louise," Beth told him, "feels that you should not see each other again."

Deac's voice came in a dangerous purr: "What damned kind of she-business have you been putting over in there, Beth?"

"I? Don't be absurd. Try using some intelligence and sensitivity." She was not annoyed. Instead, she showed rather a kindly condescension. "Surely you realize that the girl can never risk forming any attachment with the man who killed her husband, don't you? After all, whatever the circumstances, she is Arne Bassett's widow. After I broke the news to her about Arne—"

"Lady, you planted that in her head!"

Wade said hushedly, "God," and slung around and set off without purpose down the yard.

"There are things," Beth answered Deac, "that a lady knows by instinct she must not do. The girl's right. That would be wrong—for her. Thinking so would make it wrong—for her. It would drive her mad. Don't be too hard on me, Deac."

He frowned reflectively at her. His eyes unmasked a sympathy again and a sad wondering. He left her, and walked away in the purposeless direction Wade had taken.

Wade fetched up against a corral fence. He laid his hands up on the top pole, arms out stiff, and just stood there. Deac came alongside and after gazing into the corral a while he murmured, "Hurt?"

Wade rolled his head as if to clear it. "It's not always the hurt that hits a man too quick."

Deac thought that over. Presently he began talking in a flat, low voice.

"Beth's right. And you're crazy. What you've got for that girl is pity, and she's entitled to more than pity from the next man she marries. She'll get married. She'll get over all this. She's not the kind to be an old maid, and you're not the only man who'll ever want to take care of her. When she's well, and Stuart's well, we'll take her home. If there's anything twisted there, old Hugh and I will kick the kinks out. If anything's due you from there, we'll collect it for your account."

"Thanks, Deac, but—"

"Another thing. If you've got to feel all sorry for somebody, running a damned boarding house can't be much of a life. Frank Brouk's Bar V is available; and as for Gunsight, it's not likely the girl will want to claim it as Bassett's widow. So you can take your pick, with one proviso—I won't stand for any more bachelor neighbors!" Deac kicked the lower fence rail. "Anything else I can do to square the bill?"

"You could give me the loan of a horse."

"Going to town?"

"Right away."

"Help yourself."

Deac paced into the big, bare room, pulled a chair out from the table, and sat waiting. It was a few minutes before Beth came out from the bedroom where Louise lay. She glanced away from him and started to go back, evidently having thought she had heard Wade Forrest enter.

In the same low voice that he had used with Wade down at the corral, Deac said, "Lady, he's gone."

"What?" She whirled about. "What did you say?"

He lowered his eyes to the table before him. "I said he's gone."

The cumbersome skirt of her riding habit flowed swiftly into a corner of his vision. "What—do—you—mean?"

"Catherine Larmor."

He waited, waited. The folds of skirt hung still. There was no sound at all. He rose swiftly, sweeping his chair back. Refusing to see her face, he took her in his arms, pulling her close and brushing one hand up to her head and tucking it below the level of his jaw.

"Take it easy, lady. Take it easy."

She was crying against his fine white linen shirtfront.

He stroked her hair, thinking of this second shattering of her self-confidence and how it would need to be rebuilt. Some day. Maybe some day. . . .

Wade turned in his borrowed T Anchor horse at Wright's, and Jim Wright himself came from his tiny office to take it, his manner guardedly friendly. Outside again in the harsh exposure of afternoon sunshine, he cut across the main street toward the east side, on the slight angle that would take him directly to East Street.

A feeling of being conspicuous aroused an odd fancy that the main street had grown wider. The noon of violence still spread its aftermath of excited disturbance over the town. Nothing was normal. Groups remained clotted everywhere he looked—even along bad West Block, usually torpid till after dark; and good East Block whose prim neatness discouraged boardwalk idlers. Toland's big shaded gallery held a Saturday-size crowd. An air of expectancy reached out and probed every slightest occurrence as a possible augur of something more to happen.

And now they all were silent, all watching the tall, lean-built man walking alone across the street. At that moment Harrison pushed open the front door of his Emporium, stepped far out and raised a hand in greeting. Wade waved back.

It broke the unbearable stillness. It set the wind of general opinion. The ripple of movement on Toland's gallery was nothing more than a series of nods to Wade as he came near on his diagonal course, but it was enough. Maya was revising its opinion of him. In time the country would simply accept him, as it had once had to learn to accept the notorious Deac Shanter. Wade nodded gravely in return and passed on into East Street.

He entered the Larmor house through the front, and went down the length of the hall, through the dining room and into the kitchen. Katey, working alone there, stopped deliberately and looked at him. Her silence was cold.

"Where is she, Katey?"

"Who?"

"Catherine."

"Oh." A ball of white dough in brown hands slammed the bakeboard. "*Miss* Catherine is upstairs. She is not well, and does not wish to be disturbed—sir."

"Her room's the last one back, isn't it?"

No reply.

He asked, going out through the dining room, "Would you like to come out on a ranch, Katey, and cook for just three or four or five?"

He reached the hall before she called, "Wade." She was at the kitchen door, smiling her richest smile. "Man, you fix it up, you hear? Yes, last room back."

Catherine's door hung half open. Catherine lay on the bed, face down, her arms curled tightly around her fair head.

He walked in, and as soon as she raised her head and saw him, he asked, "Will you marry me?"

Her eyes regarded him enormously. "Why?"

"Hunh?" He frowned, cupping his hands out and letting them fall again. "Because I love you, dammit, why else?"

"What a way to say it!" She whirled over and sprang to the floor, and he caught her. There was a foolish moment during which her hands fumbled against his coat before curling around him under it and tugging at him. "But it'll do for now."